JIMMY THE TERRORIST

JIMMY THE TERRORIST

Omair Ahmad

HAMISH HAMILTON
an imprint of
PENGUIN BOOKS

HAMISH HAMILTON
Published by the Penguin Group
Penguin Books India Pvt. Ltd, 11 Community Centre, Panchsheel Park,
New Delhi 110 017, India
Penguin Group (USA) Inc., 375 Hudson Street, New York, New York 10014, USA
Penguin Group (Canada), 90 Eglinton Avenue East, Suite 700, Toronto,
Ontario, M4P 2Y3, Canada (a division of Pearson Penguin Canada Inc.)
Penguin Books Ltd, 80 Strand, London WC2R 0RL, England
Penguin Ireland, 25 St Stephen's Green, Dublin 2, Ireland
(a division of Penguin Books Ltd)
Penguin Group (Australia), 250 Camberwell Road, Camberwell,
Victoria 3124, Australia (a division of Pearson Australia Group Pty Ltd)
Penguin Group (NZ), 67 Apollo Drive, Rosedale, North Shore 0632,
New Zealand (a division of Pearson New Zealand Ltd)
Penguin Group (South Africa) (Pty) Ltd, 24 Sturdee Avenue, Rosebank,
Johannesburg 2196, South Africa

Penguin Books Ltd, Registered Offices: 80 Strand, London WC2R 0RL, England

First published in Hamish Hamilton by Penguin Books India 2010

Copyright © Omair Ahmad 2010

10 9 8 7 6 5 4 3 2 1

ISBN 9780670083640

This is a work of fiction. Names, characters, places and incidents are either the product
of the author's imagination or are used fictitiously and any resemblance to any actual
person, living or dead, events or locales is entirely coincidental.

Typeset in Sabon Roman by SÜRYA, New Delhi
Printed at Gopsons Papers Ltd., Noida

Abba, Amma, aap ke liye . . .

PROLOGUE

Look at them, how they gather, descending like kites upon a fresh kill.

Their feet barely touch the ground, and when they do they can only hop about, crippled. No, this isn't their kind of place. These shrill birds only look good in their air-conditioned studios in Delhi and Bombay. But they had to come, didn't they? The blood and meat are here. It doesn't matter how great or fine they are in flight, at the end of the day they have to descend to the earth to feed. Even down to the soil of this half-blighted place we call Moazzamabad.

When was the last time we saw one of their tribe, hungry for details of blood and crime? Certainly not last year, when more than a thousand died, in fever and pain, largely in poverty. Japanese encephalitis, the doctors called it, although why it was Japanese nobody knew. There is nothing foreign about people dying in Moazzamabad, so no reason to give the disease a foreign name. And Japanese? You always think of technology when you talk about Japan, not of a sickness carried by mosquitoes from buffaloes wallowing in mud and muck.

I am intrigued that you ask about our town, though what brings you here is the same news that has the press so excited. That's a good sign; maybe you'll gather more than any of these reporters will. And maybe I should tell you the boy's story after all.

Though, what can I tell you about this place? Where do we begin? There were people dying here four centuries ago, in the same poverty and dirt, when Moazzam Shah, son of the mighty Aurangzeb, marched in to put down an uprising. They wanted independence, I think, or just freedom from taxes, maybe. They received a full share of swords instead. It was part of Nepal then, not India, this forested, bandit-infested region past the Ghaghra river. Moazzam Shah came not once, but twice, and left behind both his name and a band of soldiers to keep the place under Mughal rule. The Turkmen among them founded the Turkmaanpur mohalla; the Afghans started their own little colony. But slowly the town swallowed them all, keeping the names and little else.

Delhi tried again. In a bid to raise revenue the Mughal court ordered that those who cleared any patch of forest would become owners of that land. And this was how our town acquired a Jungle Subhaan Ali, and a Jungle Vishnu Das, even a Jungle Mosley Sahib, named after a white man who arrived before the British took Delhi. He was long dead by the time they managed to extend their control here, eight hundred kilometres from the capital—though even in those days it may well have been halfway around the world.

Moazzamabad resisted the British as successfully as it had resisted the Mughals, adding a neighbourhood here, a family or two there, a few names, the occasional legend. The white men were almost all connected with the indigo plantations. They would wear Indian clothes during the week, finding comfort in local dress when other Europeans could not see them. On Sundays, though, it was stifling European formality, as they braved the heat and humidity to spend an evening getting fantastically drunk with their compatriots at the grandly titled Moazzamabad Club.

The white sahibs did not notice the brown hands or rounded features of the bearers who served them, or of the servants who helped them out of their clothes and shoes when they returned senseless late at night. And in the morning they did not notice the wheat or paddy growing in their small landholdings. They were blind, as the Mughals before them, to the vastness of the people who lived here, to their everyday prayers and fears, their suffering and resilience. Only the taxes mattered, and the five names, maybe ten, who could be useful allies or spittoons.

They cared little, the Angrez, for the Hanuman mandir that grew slowly, like a live thing, from a tiny room at the time of the great rebellion of 1857 to a towering edifice. It is ten storeys high now, the tallest building in town. Then, as now, nobody with any real understanding of power and wealth asked about matters of religion: it helped everything move smoothly if you didn't. If most of the town was Hindu, and some part of their income ended up at the temple, what did the rulers care as long as the taxmen got their due, as long as the money came on time?

Whether it was the white sahibs who ruled or the brown ones who took their place, they had no time for Moazzamabad.

Suddenly, now, the worthies in Delhi care. All those who

run this magic lantern show we call India—they especially
care. This time there was no choice, this time they had to
notice, and the vultures had to swoop down, as Moazzam
Shah had done long ago. They had been screaming about
terrorists for so long that when Moazzamabad presented
one of its own, a boy called Jimmy, how could it be
ignored? It is dramatic enough for the newspapers, for TV
even, as the many thousands of deaths in the last four
hundred years never were.

Oh, I don't doubt their good intentions—one must never
doubt their good intentions. But you see, I have no faith in
it all any more. What will they find? Jimmy is the end of
a long story, and nobody cares for those today. Two
headlines, a photo, and before you know it we will be
talking about cricket, maybe Bollywood. Probably both.

One of the press-walas was asking for house number
1593. The fool. This is not a place of numbers, but names.
Just a glance at the muddle of buildings will tell you that.
Not one of them has a house number, and many sprawl
into each other, spilling over their boundaries and merging,
just as the families who live in them have done over
generations. Ask the residents of our town and they would
be hard put to tell you how they are named in the
government records, much less the number that the
government has assigned to their homes.

Even the name of this mohalla, Rasoolpur, finds no
place in official parlance. But that is what it is, named after
Qazi Mohammed Murtaza Rasool, a wandering mendicant
who decided, for reasons nobody really knows, to stop his

journeying under the shade of a tree by a river three
hundred years ago.

The tree is long gone, and the river that once ran clear
and sparkling to the sea is a sewage canal. The only reason
anybody would stop here now would be if they were
overwhelmed by the stink of rotting garbage. This is a
forgotten place. But everybody in Moazzamabad knows
that this is Rasoolpur, and everybody knows about the tree
by the river. Just as they know about Shabbir Manzil, grand
and incongruous for this town, though a little rundown.

You don't see it? Sorry. I had forgotten how they have
built all around it. Just there, behind that tyre shop, and
the clinic—do you see the rising edge of that roof? That's
Shabbir Manzil, the real reason why our mohalla is famous.
(You didn't really think anybody would remember a
wandering mendicant, did you?) Legend has it that the
family came from Basra, in what is now Iraq, but then was
magnificent Persia. They came to teach the royal families
of Jaunpur how to conduct themselves with dignity, what
to read, how to converse. But as luck would have it, the
royal family decided to become Shia, and the Shabbirs
found themselves confronted with a difficult choice: to
convert as well, or to keep to their Sunni faith. One branch
converted. The other, hearing of the Mughal offer to clear
forest for grants of land, made for Moazzamabad.

Clearing the land was simple. You just paid others to do
it. But living here was difficult, especially for those of
refined tastes, as the Shabbirs thought themselves to be. By
their very nature they wanted to guide, to instruct, to lead;

but you can't lead if you have no one to follow you. The Mughals wielded the only power in those days—lackadaisically, yes, but if you have too much power and for too long, you only need to do things after a fashion. Things come to you, people bow to you, it just happens, till the burden of privilege becomes too heavy to bear and whole empires, like ordinary men, self-destruct . . . But that is another story.

Coming back to the Shabbirs, power was not to their interest, culture was. However, the town was largely Hindu, and in matters of culture and ritual, people turned to the Hanuman mandir—for leadership, for song and dance, for saints and ascetics. The few leaders sent by the Mughals reported that the descendants of the Afghans and the Turkmen, not deeply attached to their faith to begin with, had also fallen under the sway of the *kafir* saints and madmen.

In such a place the memory of the Muslim pir Qazi Mohammed Murtaza Rasool was of great use to the Shabbirs. Careful not to trespass against the ban on saint worship in their orthodox Sunni tradition, they honoured him instead with a week-long prayer meeting, just after the Milad-en-Nabi, when Prophet Mohammed's birthday was celebrated with great fanfare by the Afghans and Turkmen in typically barbarous fashion. Over years, decades, generations, the men of Shabbir Manzil became the spokesmen of their community, the carriers of memory and tradition. They became the ones who taught the Muslims of this little mohalla in a vast Hindu sea how to behave, how to be Muslim, but lightly, with more culture and pride than hard faith. The Shabbirs spoke for and on behalf of the Muslims of Moazzamabad with the Mughals first, the British next and the inheritors of the Raj—our newly minted brown sahibs—afterwards.

Everyone knows that.

Just as everyone knows that there was nobody named Jimmy in Moazzamabad, just a young man named Jamaal Ansari, son of Rafiq Ansari and Shaista Shabbir, who prepared the long road their child would one day take.

And if you know that, then maybe you know everything . . .

Yes, that's the story these microphone- and camera-happy fools must trace if they hope to understand anything.

They must go all the way back to Rafiq and Shaista. Why should it be surprising that a son looks up to his father, and lives forever in his shadow? Where is the mystery in the fact that women do more than simply accept a man's seed; that mothers shape their children inside them for nine months and for a lifetime outside? Neither Rafiq nor Shaista was strange, neither was cursed—or blessed, if you like—with extraordinariness. How then could Jamaal be so different, this sudden monster that he's become, this Jimmy the terrorist?

Because of this, at least, there can be no doubt: whatever Jimmy was, whatever Jamaal became, in the end he was their son, Rafiq's and Shaista's, and their story. And because their story played out in Rasoolpur, he was also the story of this mohalla. And of Shabbir Manzil.

None of the reporters have gone there yet. They are not welcome, nor do they know that they should have asked.

It would have been hard to imagine that in Rafiq's time. Ever since it was built, and till recently, Shabbir Manzil was the place where outsiders came, where they were informed or entertained. It was the hub around which the mohalla revolved. Rafiq was no different from most other men of his time, hungry to be acknowledged, and he knew that the only acknowledgement that mattered in his neighbourhood was to be recognized at Shabbir Manzil . . .

Maybe if he hadn't had that small hunger, none of this would have come to pass.

BOOK ONE

1

All those years ago, when he was still looking for his first job, Rafiq Ansari never cared more about anything than what was being discussed at Shabbir Manzil. Since joining college in 1965, his greatest ambition had been to have tea there, to sit among the notables of Rasoolpur mohalla and speak of poetry and cricket, perhaps make a learned comment, but casually, on some bit of politics that had recently made its way into the newspapers.

In a way it was not his fault. He was the youngest amongst his brothers, and his parents, wanting to give him a leg-up in society, had sent him to St Jude's. Although this wasn't as prestigious as being sent to Lucknow or Delhi, or the swank boarding schools set up in the hill stations by the British, an education at St Jude's meant something in Moazzamabad. It was at St Jude's that Rafiq had learned that success was a small thing, social standing was the greater goal, and in Rasoolpur only one house determined where you stood in the ranks of society: Shabbir Manzil.

Rafiq pursued this ambition with single-minded devotion, climbing above his station, marrying beyond his means, turning away from opportunities that would take him far from Moazzamabad and lose him the chance to make the one remark that would draw praise from all around him, and would be savoured by the caretakers of culture for a generation or more.

It was no easy thing to achieve. There were many guardians on the path to such eminence, great egos to be propitiated, small men to be praised, and always the need to make it all seem that he wasn't trying too hard. Nothing would doom his chances so completely as to be known as an upstart aspiring to social recognition.

Turning down a job with the Indian Railways, Rafiq idled, a pursuit that only the sons of the rich could afford. He called it studying: he had done not just his MA, but a BEd as well, telling his parents all the while that there was a great career in education—weren't the vice chancellors of Indian universities all great men? To be a professor was to be on the pathway to power. And his father, who had only studied up to the tenth grade, who already had a son who was an engineer and a second who was a lawyer, and who knew, all the while, what Rafiq was made of, didn't protest too much.

But after his BEd, Rafiq had to live up to his boasts, and found that he could not. And then, after six months of increasingly elaborate excuses, when even his mother mentioned something about working to feed himself, he had the good fortune to be almost run over by Ahmed Saeed Shabbir's jeep.

'Arre Rafiq!' Ahmed Saeed exclaimed in the plum tones

befitting the eldest son of the most prominent family in the mohalla, the only one who was a member of the Lions Club and who had dinner at the District Magistrate's house, whose hands had so little need of work that they were softer than the calfskin shoes that he ordered from a shop in Kanpur whose name nobody in Moazzamabad knew.

'Arre Rafiq! *Kaise behke behke chal rahe ho*? You haven't fallen in love now, have you, my boy?'

The horn had startled Rafiq but he didn't care. In all his years Ahmed Saeed had never addressed him, never in such a tone, almost as if he was talking to an equal. And Rafiq wasn't about to let the opportunity pass. Though what should he say, and how? Only the rich fell in love, even he knew that, only the rich and the desperately poor could afford to. The closest that Rafiq was likely to come to romance was copying Rajesh Khanna's hairstyle.

Thinking furiously, but determined not to show it, Rafiq ignored the glare that Rustam, Ahmed Saeed's bulldog of a driver, threw his way. It was that glance that cleared his brain and, assuming a jaunty tone that went well with his superstar haircut, he replied, 'One can also *rise* in love, Ahmed Saeed sahib, not just fall in it—unless brought down to earth by the honking of a car horn.'

Ahmed Saeed guffawed at the well-turned phrase, and Rafiq, who had been worried that he might be going a little too far with the implied criticism, relaxed and laughed along.

'Jump in, Majnu,' Ahmed Saeed said, 'let me drop you off at your house. We can't let lovers be run over by careless drivers now, can we?'

As Rafiq moved to jump into the rear of the jeep, Ahmed Saeed said, 'Not back there, old man, there's enough space in the front.'

Things changed that evening for Rafiq. What an honour it was to be riding with Ahmed Saeed, in the front seat at that, shoulder to shoulder with the most important man in the mohalla. He could hear the buzz of gossip subside and rise as they passed by tea shop after tea shop, and knew that everybody was watching them. One of Rafiq's friends had the temerity to wave, and Rafiq's face crinkled in distaste. He only partially raised a hand to acknowledge the greeting.

'Who was that?' Ahmed Saeed wanted to know.

'Oh, Ahmed Saeed sahib,' Rafiq said, laughing dismissively, 'you know how it is these days, everybody thinks they are your equals. That young man is in his third year of engineering and thinks that makes him fit to have conversations with this *nacheez* who was mad enough to keep at it till he'd done an MA, and a BEd too.'

'Really?' Ahmed Saeed sounded a little bewildered. He hadn't realized that somebody of Rafiq's class could actually claim to be educated.

'First class,' Rafiq said, and then clarified, 'although they didn't give it to me in my BEd for a two-mark difference.'

'They must have realized that you are Muslim,' Ahmed Saeed said grumpily.

It seemed implausible. The examination papers went to the central examination board, and there were no names on the papers, only identification numbers. But Rafiq nodded along. Everybody knew that Ahmed Saeed had managed to pass the fiendishly difficult civil service exam three times, only to be denied at the interview stage. Three times he had faced a board of examiners armed with the air of a man accustomed to power and privilege, with the knowledge that all that was best in India could be his, and three times he had been denied by the stony faced men. It had been years since those slights, but Ahmed Saeed still brooded on them, assigning many reasons for his failure to break into the privileged club of Indian bureaucracy.

Ahmed Saeed had lapsed into silence, but just before they reached Rafiq's house, he seemed to come out of his sudden despondency. 'Come to my house tomorrow. If you're free, that is.'

Rafiq had a job interview the next day, but this was an invitation to Shabbir Manzil. 'The British are gone,' he said, waving a hand, 'we're all free men now.'

Ahmed Saeed laughed. 'Good man,' he said and squeezed Rafiq's thigh, a gesture that could only mean that they were now friends.

Rafiq walked into his parents' house with his chest stuck out, knowing that things were going to change, that they had already changed, that he was a man of promise. He woke up early the next day, so early that he managed to make it for the pre-dawn prayers at the neighbourhood mosque, something he hadn't done in years. But the sleepy devout who were about so early in the morning were not the ones that Rafiq could speak to about Shabbir Manzil. And of course Ahmed Saeed wasn't there—even though it was his great-grandfather who had financed the building of the mosque about a hundred years ago. It was well known that Ahmed Saeed woke only after eleven in the morning and wouldn't see anyone before noon.

'Rafiq beta,' the maulvi called out as Rafiq sat at the doorway of the mosque struggling to pull on his shoes. They were just a little small for him, and bit into his ankles if he walked too far in them, but he considered them his lucky pair—and he had polished them lovingly the night before, humming happily to himself, enjoying the smell of the Cherry polish and the deep shine that the leather acquired.

'As salaam aleikum Maulana sahib,' Rafiq said, as he finally succeeded with the shoes, 'how have you been?'

'Alhamdulillah, Praise be to God,' the maulvi replied, 'it's been ages since I have seen you here.'

Even to Rafiq, with his finely tuned ear for both praise and censure, there was no criticism in those words. Maulana Jalali Qayoom was a kindly man, and it showed on his round face with its curiously Central Asian features.

'I'm running around trying to get a job, Maulana sahib,' Rafiq said, and then, looking up at Qayoom sahib, he asked abruptly, 'Will you pray for me?'

The maulvi reached out and patted Rafiq on the cheek. 'Always. My prayers are with you children, always.'

And as Rafiq turned to go, he added, 'Think of marriage as well, beta, once you have the job.'

Rafiq nodded, but although he had been questioned repeatedly about marriage—he was almost thirty and both

his brothers had married before they turned twenty-five—
that day the maulvi's quiet words had a deeper impact.
Rafiq would think of them later, wondering whether the
maulvi had mixed up the prayers, or combined them both
as some kind of package deal—a toothbrush free with a
tube of toothpaste.

It was a long day for Rafiq, made longer by the unusual
edge of anticipation. It had been years, more than a
decade, since he had looked forward to an event. Nothing
much happened in Moazzamabad; or if it did, none of it
mattered to the denizens of Rasoolpur. Of course people
still followed cricket matches on their transistor radios, but
that was no longer Rafiq's style.

He cancelled the job interview in the evening. It had
been nothing much, a clerical position in the forestry
department, and he hadn't been keen on it anyway. But he
didn't tell his parents. His father was pleasantly surprised
by the particularity with which Rafiq ironed his clothes,
fussing over the lightest crease, and gave him a little money
for the rickshaw so that his shiny shoes wouldn't scuff.
Rafiq almost blurted out the truth then, but he bit down
the words. He was convinced that his family would not
understand the significance of Shabbir Manzil—how could
they, with their limited education and their modest, middle-
class background? Now was not the time to enlighten
them.

When Rafiq stopped the rickshaw just before Shabbir
Manzil he was all set to confront the gathering there, but

as he made his way down the long driveway he saw that
there was nobody sitting in the courtyard. Was he too
early? Had there been a misunderstanding?

His stomach tightened suddenly. What would he tell his
father?

Just as he rounded the final bend, Rafiq spotted Rustam
polishing the old Buick that had been acquired by the old
Shabbir sahib nearly forty years ago, and which was rarely
taken out on the broken roads of Moazzamabad.

'Rustam,' Rafiq said, 'Ahmed Saeed sahib had called
me.'

It was an unnecessary thing to say; Rustam had been
right there, in the jeep with them, last evening, and he had
heard the invitation clearly enough.

'His bhaijaan is here,' Rustam said sourly, 'his cousin
from Lucknow.'

And then as Rafiq stood, caught unprepared, Rustam
added, 'There'll be no gathering today.'

The humiliation, and that too at the hands of a servant,
brought the blood rising to Rafiq's face. If a mere driver
mocked him like this, what would the others say?

'Tell him I'm here,' Rafiq said sharply, his voice slightly
screechy.

When Rustam made to protest, Rafiq cut him off: 'Tell
him. Now.'

Rustam looked him up and down lazily, then dropped
the rag he was holding on the bonnet of the Buick, and
walked into the doorway of the mouldering old house.

As he waited, Rafiq's anger subsided a little, only to

come rushing back when he imagined how the others would laugh at this.

And then suddenly came the booming voice of Ahmed Saeed: 'Arre Rafiq, forgive me, it had completely slipped my mind that you were coming today, but it's good that you came.'

Rafiq stretched his hand to take Ahmed Saeed's, careful not to grip it too hard. Ahmed Saeed's soft, large hand tightened briefly and then fell out of his grip.

'Have you met Ismat sahib?' Ahmed Saeed said, gesturing to the tall, cadaverous figure standing next to him.

This time Rafiq's hand was taken in a firm, bony grip. The tall man's skin was dry and coarse, and he held Rafiq's hand for longer than seemed necessary, looking at him searchingly.

'*As salaam aleikum,*' Ismat sahib said finally in a low voice.

'*Wa aleikum as salaam,*' Rafiq replied, and Ismat sahib nodded.

'Come in, come in,' Ahmed Saeed put a hand on Rafiq's shoulder, turning him towards the house. Ismat sahib fell in on the other side, flanking Rafiq.

'I was just telling Ismat bhaijaan about your qualities. We were discussing Sir S.A. Alvi College, since I serve on the managing committee. They're starting a geography department, and there are a few jobs. It would be a good place for a young man with capabilities such as yours to start out.'

'I studied history,' Rafiq clarified.

'Close enough, close enough,' Ahmed Saeed said heartily. 'You have a first-class degree in the arts. That's what matters, educational excellence. The rest is a matter of detail.'

Rafiq felt his chest swell, and then Ismat sahib's hand settled on his other shoulder.

'In fact,' Ahmed Saeed said, 'it will also give you the chance to meet Ismat sahib's sister. Shaista will also be joining the college. She passed first class as well.'

'With distinction,' Ismat sahib added softly, as if reminded of something he had tried to forget but failed.

The wedding took place only a few months later.

2

Was it her fault?

It's hard even to think that, quiet as she was, with such few joys in life, and now so long dead. She loved him dearly, her *lal*. The moon of her delight, she would call him, and it was true that he was the fulfilment of her dreams, to the extent that she had any dreams left to cherish by the time he was born.

It is hard to think of her in that way, of her hand in his death, her own, uncertain love dragging her to the grave and he following not too long after, like the obedient child he was.

Who could accuse Shaista of anything, other than an inordinate love for her child? And which Indian mother can be accused of anything less?

Her life, as far back as could be recalled, had been an increasingly tightening spiral into deprivation and silence. It had bruised her, perhaps hardened her a little, long before she came to live in our mohalla. She wasn't born poor, nor did she ever reach the state of destitution that millions around us suffer but few of us will ever understand.

It was relentless dispossession, a slide into near penury, that cut off each and every avenue to the wider world. In the little casbah of Tufailganj, barely a dozen kilometres from Lucknow, she had lived minutes away from the capital of Uttar Pradesh, the centre of power for more than a hundred and fifty million souls. A city of graceful architecture and learned gatherings, full of colleges and with a university of its own, Lucknow fled away from her day by day, year after year.

Shaista was barely thirteen when her father passed away, a year after her mother's death. It was a shock but she was young, and it took only a little while for her to recover, or pretend to, and return to dreams of college, of new clothes and the adoration of young boys from good families that should have been her birthright. Then her brother Ismat, her hero, who was a decade and a half older and almost a second father, came to see her late one morning at her school. It was a convent school, some seventy years old, famed for its discipline and discretion, where people of means sent their daughters to study. In the six years that Shaista had been there, neither her father nor, after him, her brother had ever needed to come to the school. Shaista was surprised but delighted to see her Bhaijaan that morning.

In the empty visiting room, Ismat sat her down and after checking that the door was locked, said, 'We cannot afford to pay for your school fees.'

'Bhaijaan,' she said, bowing her head, uncomprehending.

'Bitiya,' he said, using the diminutive that their father had used, 'Bitiya, I'm sorry.'

It was the weariness in his voice that breached her defences and she started to cry, weeping silently. He waited, wishing she would only understand and not ask him anything. But she did. 'Can I . . .' she began, and then stopped until she could summon up the energy to continue, 'Can I say goodbye to my friends?'

Ismat rose abruptly, turned and crossed the room. His voice was gruff, and she knew he was hiding tears. 'There are three months until the summer holidays. We have enough for that, and enough that you can finish your tenth class exams next year as a correspondence student. You can be an external student of the school after that, if you do well. I have spoken to the headmistress and she said it is possible.'

And because she was fourteen, she rushed across the room and hugged him, babbling her thanks and weeping into his sherwani. He patted her gently on the head, and shushed her, saying, 'Bitiya. Bitiya.'

He could have asked anything in the world of her after that, and she would have agreed. But really, what did she have that she could give him? She couldn't stop the declining price of sugar cane, or the creeping encroachments by small farmers onto their farmlands and small orchards. She had no power to make the officials at the land registry department less corrupt, or the poor-quality farm equipment more efficient. She could not argue with the banks that refused to give Ismat a loan to bore a well he so desperately needed. She couldn't advise him about the right insecticide to use on the mango trees, or stop tree rot from killing the crops in the first two seasons alone. And when he had finally figured things out—identified which of the farm hands were thieving scum and which were merely stupid, and which tractor driver would actually do some work and which one would only use the diesel money to drink himself into an incoherent rage, pick a fight and end up in jail with the tractor impounded; when he had learned the names and patterns of the seasons and could tell the different varieties of rice by the smell and feel of the grain alone—by the time her Bhaijaan had acquired all these skills, she could do nothing about the two years of drought that hit eastern Uttar Pradesh, driving better farmers than him into destitution.

All that Shaista could do was study. She couldn't even run the household, and had to quietly watch as her sister-in-law bought a new set of clothes and earrings and shoes every time she left for her family home, carrying expensive gifts for her brothers and sisters, while Ismat hoarded his clothes, using them sparely, and had his father's sherwanis altered to fit him.

Shaista understood her fate after the results of her twelfth class exams. She had done well, even as an external student, and the headmistress of her school was kind enough to send a personal letter inviting her to the ceremony where they would honour the three top-scoring students.

She was so excited that she could barely sleep the night before, and got up three times to check the shalwar suit that she had washed and ironed for the occasion. It was almost new. She had worn it only twice before, and had carefully packed it away after she left school, treasuring it as a memory of what she had once been.

On the day, it fitted her perfectly. Even her sharp-tongued sister-in-law complimented her on how the light blue of the cloth suited her fair skin. But it was at school that the truth came out. Fashion is cruel and ever changing, and the style had changed drastically in a year and a half. The tops were now shorter and tighter, and the pyjamas flared wide at the ankles. Shaista in her old-fashioned suit sat like a dowdy aunt of a bygone era and, when she was called on stage to accept her certificate from the principal, she felt the gaze of all her former classmates, looking at her with pity.

It was Muniza, light-hearted, happy Muniza, whose only sadness was an unrequited passion for the filmstar Manoj Kumar and a tendency to plumpness, who completed the destruction, as only well-meaning friends can. 'Shazoo, how are you? Where have you been hiding?' And then, looking Shaista up and down, she added, 'And you're amazing. I think you fit better into that suit than when you bought it with me at Halwasia Market. *How* do you do it?'

Shaista tried to answer, to keep her composure. She loved Muniza, and knew how innocent the remark was, but the blood had already rushed to her face, and now as she tried to say something, anything, all she managed was a half-choked sob.

Muniza immediately became concerned. 'Shazoo, are you all right?'

By this time Shaista knew that she wasn't all right,

would never be all right, and the tears wouldn't stop. She kissed Muniza and, grabbing Ismat's sleeve, left her friends behind forever.

At home she packed away the clothes of her childhood, and if her sister-in-law dressed up Shaista held her tongue. Ismat had given her three precious months, had given her pride and allowed her to leave the convent with her head held high. So now she kept it bowed low over her books. The days of clothes and fashion and attention from suitable boys pretending at heart-stopping love were over for her. The only things she could earn were the laurels of academia, and maybe some freedom there. She did well in her college, and excellently in her MA.

There were sweets the day her results were declared. Ismat brought them with him with the newspaper that carried the results. And the greatest delight for Shaista, although she could not say it, was that her sister-in-law was visiting her parents. Shaista didn't have to be polite, or even humble. 'First class!' she marvelled, holding the newspaper in a tight grip.

'With distinction, Bitiya,' Ismat said, laughing his slow, deep laugh. 'How many external students have ever received a first class with distinction?'

She took a breath, turned to face him, and said, 'I want to teach, Bhaijaan.'

And that was enough to silence his laughter. He didn't answer at first, just wiped away the bit of kaju barfi that clung at the corner of his mouth with a handkerchief. Then he slowly lowered his angular frame into one of the four overstuffed chairs in the drawing room. He was leaning forward, looking at the faded carpet, so that his face was hidden from her. All she could see were the veins and tendons that stood out when he clasped his hands. 'You don't have to work, Bitiya, haven't I taken care of you all these years?'

'I'd like to teach,' she repeated, but not so insistent that she would hurt him.

'It's just this year,' Ismat said. 'Once this is gone, we will start planning your wedding. I promise.'

But when she was silent, not saying anything, he knew that it wasn't agreement that kept her quiet. Slowly he raised his head so that she could see the anger on his face.

'Wait a year,' he said flatly.

Still she didn't speak.

And he burst out, 'What do you want to become, a nun?' He couldn't stop himself after that, and continued in rage, 'Or do you want to become like those schoolteachers with their ugly saris, their rough hands and their loud laughter, those women that have no future except to become spinsters or worse!'

She held herself back from saying it, but she was twenty-four years old now—already close to being a spinster by the calculations of all those around her. But he must have understood her. Hadn't she been silent so long, and hadn't he understood that silence all along?

'I know I've failed you, Bitiya,' he said bitterly, lowering his eyes. 'I know that you deserved more from your brother, from life, from the inheritance that we received, but what more could I do?'

She couldn't stand that, not from her beloved brother who had done everything for her, and she walked over to sit on the sofa next to him. With a hand on his shoulder, she said, 'You haven't failed me, Bhaijaan. Abbu and Ammi would have been proud of you. But you can't keep me here forever.'

He refused to look at her, or to answer.

'There are colleges as well, Bhaijaan,' she said, not wishing to argue, trying to make things easier for him. 'I could teach there instead, if you feel that a school would be too rough.'

It was a silly statement. Why would a college hire her, when she had no experience, just a degree—however fine it might be—with nobody to put in a word for her at a hiring committee? There were many more schools and she would have a far better chance with them.

Ismat turned to her, and said fiercely, 'If you won't give me a year, at least give me three months.'

What could she do but agree? She wasn't in a position to refuse him anything. The only thing she could give, or withhold, were her prayers. So she kissed his right hand, and said, 'My life has always been in your hands, for you to do with it as you wish.'

It took him four months, though, to find her the job at the Sir S.A. Alvi College in Moazzamabad. But that was not all that he had been searching for, or all that he found. He also found Rafiq, in whose hands he entrusted Shaista, a gift so large that Rafiq had no idea what to do with it.

3

It might have been rebellion, what happened next. It might have been Shaista laying claim to her life and her own pleasure at long last, casting aside all the rules and codes that had bound her for so long.

Or was it something much simpler, so truly simple that nobody could have understood, even if they knew? Something as natural as a young woman discovering the pleasure of her own body, the joy of her muscles, the lustre of her skin, the taste of her sweat? We cannot tell now: Rafiq had not the courage to ask, and Shaista kept her own counsel.

Not that she was as silent as she had been before. Something changed for Shaista with her marriage. It was not immediately obvious. Nobody would have noticed anything different when they saw her at the wedding ceremony, demure and hidden under the heavy weight of the embroidered and brocaded dupatta, with her slim hennaed hands the only bit of skin that could be seen. They would have been hard put to identify anything particularly significant in her tear-streaked face as she bid farewell to her brother. She behaved as any other bride did, sitting through every little ceremony and process that transformed her, for those few moments, into the ideal that the whole of society, like the two families, celebrated. If she was quieter than most, well, that was in character.

The change came later—two weeks after the wedding, ten days after the painful process of her first experience of sex. That first coupling was marked by no small amount of clumsiness matched by, if anything, a curious gentleness on Rafiq's part, a gentleness that bordered almost on apology. (Would our story have turned out different had he loved a woman before this, with his heart or even his body alone? Who can tell? If you ask my opinion, I would say not. But let us leave that for another time ...) Imagine Rafiq's surprise, then, when only a few days later he felt Shaista move against him, her body blindly seeking his. Later she would hold him, guiding his body, moderating his movements, shaping him to her pleasure, teaching him rhythm and complexity, and to understand what each half-articulated sound that she made—the hiss, the gasp, the half-sigh—meant. Her body would flatten against his in bed, one foot rubbing against him, pulling him closer, her stomach touching lightly against his own.

It was not love. She never murmured his name, not in all the soft and secret sounds she made. She never reached for his face, never once mumbled words of encouragement or desire in his ear. Her face was always turned away, even her hands would lie flat and open next to her on the bed at the start, only clenching and grasping the sheets as the rest of her body rose and stretched, reacted to the caress of his fingers, to the dry touch of his lips at the nape of her neck.

Or maybe it was love. But not for him.

For all his petty vanities, or maybe because of them, Rafiq had a very fine ability to detect appreciation, and there was none of that in Shaista. There was only pleasure, the making of it and the partaking of it. It was something she wanted, something she enjoyed, something that opened her body to the world, that allowed her to breathe freely, to sleep soundly, to sigh her freedom with no thought except of her own satisfaction. When she guided him, as she made her way to the particular place she needed to go, he was only an outsider, necessary but, in the end, incidental to the process. The path she took was not one where she went with him, but alone. It took her somewhere inside of herself.

He could not go there with her, he was not welcome.

During the day, in the hours of sunlight, he thought of speaking about it to her, but that kind of courage was beyond him, had always been. There were no examples for him to follow, in the mohalla or even in all of Moazzamabad. Who spoke of desire in that place, and a woman's desire at that? Such a topic would have raised snickers and sly glances, would have opened his name up to the taint of infamy, would have meant that Rafiq, foolish, foolish Rafiq, who was so close to achieving his dreams, would have them shattered in a burst of mockery that he would never be able to live down.

Oh yes, there were those who fancied themselves as ladies' men, even in Moazzamabad there were those who boasted of their conquests in bed. But what did such conquests really amount to—the bedding of a servant girl, a tumble in the hay with some farmer's smelly daughter on a patch of land that didn't deserve the name any longer, but still called itself an estate?

Men of power with great landed estates at their command could have dancing girls perform at their pleasure, could patronize poets and singers in their kothas, and the taint would only enhance the standing that they enjoyed. Those were men who asserted their power by mocking the rules that held the rest in their place. They were insulated from the consequences of their crimes. But these latter-day zamindars—what were they with their two-dozen acres of land that the law allowed them, and maybe a few acres more hidden behind the name of some cousin or other? What was their power? Where was the glory when an angry peasant stabbed Farhad Nizami in his bed, the same bed in which Farhad had tangled his legs with those of the peasant's wife?

A grubby end to a grubby man.

Very early on in his life Rafiq had understood that he did not wish to be counted among these men. Even Ahmed Saeed's younger brother, Shakeel, with his inflamed eyes, could not escape the ignominy that such deeds eventually brought. It mattered little that his family still maintained a measure of power with their row upon row of shops in the centre of town, with their sugar mill, and the profits from Tasveer Mahal, Moazzamabad's first, and still its most respectable, movie theatre. It didn't even make a difference that his excursions took place in Lucknow, some three hundred kilometres away. The scandal came back to Moazzamabad like a scent on his skin that would not leave him, that would mark him out at every gathering.

No wife ever accompanied her husband to Shakeel sahib's house, and no child was allowed to go to his door, not even on Eid, to greet him on that auspicious day.

The world had changed after the British left, had started changing even before that. Now a man could not indulge his desire without paying the price. But a woman's desire, when had that ever been discussed? Did such a thing even exist outside the pages of the smutty English novels with lingerie-clad women posing suggestively along the barrel of a gun? And even if it did, was a married woman, of a good family, allowed to exercise it, right here in Moazzamabad?

It was a baffling question, far beyond Rafiq. The world was not what he had imagined it to be. But at least one thing gave him comfort, and that was the company of the other men who would gather every day at Shabbir Manzil, and they too would discuss change, talking of a new world that was coming into being, one that was turning out to be wholly different from what they had imagined it would be.

By this time Rafiq was a member of good standing at the evening gatherings at Shabbir Manzil. He had a job, and a respectable job at that—one that didn't require that he work too hard, or sweat, and which paid him a salary modest enough for him not to forget his station. And he had married well—too well, many had thought to themselves, until the true extent, or lack thereof, of Ismat Sharif's fortunes had been revealed. The expenses of the marriage had been borne largely by Ahmed Saeed, the

Omair Ahmad

large banquet held in the lawns of Shabbir Manzil. Rafiq's parents had had to rent a wedding hall to host the walima feast afterwards, and of course it was a little gauche and the members of the Shabbir household had sat in their own corner, sniffing genteelly at this and that, too polite to express their discomfort openly.

The great surprise had been the arrival of the elderly Shabbir sahib, Ahmed Saeed's father, who was also Shaista's maternal uncle, in the gleaming Buick. The short driveway was too tight for the car, and while people shouted for a cart to be pushed aside, a chair to be moved, a scooter to be tilted at an angle, Shabbir sahib peremptorily ordered Rustam to stop the car right there in the middle of the street, blocking all traffic, as he struggled out of the back seat. Old age had bent his spine, but he still towered over most of the people there as he made his way to the podium where the married couple was seated.

Rafiq saw Shabbir sahib hobbling towards them and tried to rise, pulling the uncomprehending Shaista by the hand, but Shabbir sahib gestured for them to sit. It was Ismat Sharif who held Shabbir sahib's arm as the old man slowly climbed the three small steps to the podium. Shabbir sahib leaned over Shaista and kissed the top of her head. '*Jeeti raho*, beta,' he said. 'It's been many years since my sister left for Lucknow, and we have seen nothing of you since she died. Welcome home.'

A three-room area was cleared in one wing of Shabbir Manzil and made ready for the newly-weds, and they moved in immediately.

Rafiq's place at the evening sessions was guaranteed, even if there were a few caveats. It was understood that his previous associations were not welcome. Whatever lessons he might have learned in the life he had lived before his sudden change of fortune were irrelevant, even a little distasteful. Nobody needed to be reminded that the lords of Shabbir Manzil had chosen to marry off one of their girls to a man from a family of no real background. People would be giving their daughters in marriage to their servants next. In fact, it was understood that Rafiq had not really existed before the marriage, his life only beginning when he had taken a ride in Ahmed Saeed's jeep. He had no friends before that, only acquaintances, maybe even friendly acquaintances, but no one you could call a friend, or invite into your house. Why, even his brothers had never quite appreciated him. And how could they, when Rafiq's own parents had not understood his true worth, how he was a prodigal, a one-in-a-thousand fluke of a gentleman born in the wrong circumstances?

With no past worth mentioning, it was also understood that Rafiq could never have the first word, or the last. What could he truly say to begin a conversation? It was not his station to muse on the strange ways of the universe, considering he was part of that mystery. And anything he said could always be put better, could always be declaimed more forcefully by the others who had sat in those gatherings at Shabbir Manzil for years, learning the subtle changes of social status, refining their ability to recognize the signs of an imminent fall from grace by that one seemingly casual remark, that one seeming oversight, the accident that had been planned so precisely that there could be no escape at all.

The most that Rafiq could do was nod along, say 'Wah, wah' in appreciation at some mot juste, but not too loudly, and if he was very lucky indeed, offer the correct verse from the poet that one of the elders was trying to recall unsuccessfully.

Truth be told, Rafiq was a ready accomplice in this crime, which robbed him of family and old friends, which stole from him his history and home. It seemed like a minor theft, or even a kind of deliverance. If all the things he had secretly been ashamed of, but which he had never had the audacity to discard before, were being taken from him, he would let it happen. Neither his conscience nor his courage were overly taxed. We're all guilty of such betrayals and cowardice—in our little towns as much in your big cities. How else do we carry on . . .

And really, even if Rafiq had the nerve, the shamelessness, to speak, was this the right time? His condition was a small matter. Great changes were taking place. At Shabbir Manzil Rafiq finally heard about the riots. He had read about them in the newspapers, heard the news stories on the radio. And one day he asked the question.

For some reason Lal Sahib had not turned up that day, and with the one Hindu of the gathering missing, maybe Ahmed Saeed was freer with his words than he would have been. Or maybe it had something to do with the rise of Manoj Tripathi, the head priest at the Hanuman mandir. In a recent interview he had said that the name of

Moazzamabad should be changed to Methi, a good old Indian name that carried no trace of the time when the Mughals ruled India. The British had been thrown out, and now it was time to show the Muslims their place.

It was hard to tell whether the last bit were Tripathi's own words, or just the conclusion that the journalist had made in reporting the interview, but it was all that everybody had been discussing for the last two weeks.

'Do you know about Jabalpur?' Ahmed Saeed asked heavily.

Rafiq shook his head, although he did know that there had been a big riot there some years ago.

'That year, 1961,' Ahmed Saeed continued, 'I was in Aligarh Muslim University, doing my LLB, in my third year. The first Hindu–Muslim riot since Partition, the newspapers called it. More than a thousand people killed.'

He shook his head. 'We were caught completely unawares. Until that time all the riots had been about language, about creating Tamil Nadu and Andhra Pradesh, about breaking up Bombay State into Gujarat and Maharashtra. We'd got so used to riots about language and creating new states that we had almost forgotten that you could be killed for religion as well.

'And you know what it was all about—or at least officially? A Muslim had married a Hindu. For this more than a thousand people had bled their life out on the streets of Jabalpur.'

As Ahmed Saeed spoke, his voice gathered strength and anger, which was unusual for a man of his temperament.

Everyone was quiet. 'The government gave compensation, but our university decided to send money as well. We gathered three lakhs, and I was among the people who accompanied the team. I can't tell you what it was like. There were houses that had been dynamited, while right next to them, separated by just a wall, would be a shop that was untouched. You could walk down a street and tell which shops had been owned by Muslims—they had all been burnt down. Gutted. I met this old woman who had a lump of copper that she was trying to sell. They told me later that she had been one of the richest people in her neighbourhood, but now all her sons were dead, her house burnt down, and that lump of copper was all she had, all that remained of her kitchen utensils.'

'Why didn't the government do anything?' Rafiq asked.

'The government?' Ahmed Saeed almost spat. 'Who do you think had done it, if not the government?'

'Not Nehru?' Rafiq said, almost whispering his incredulity.

Ahmed Saeed threw up his arms in frustration. 'Who knows?'

After a moment he added, 'No, I don't think it was Nehru's doing, but those were Congress ministers who managed it all. And Nehru did nothing. On All India Radio all that could be heard were his mumbled words— something about his head being bowed by the shame of it. Such shame he must have felt, we thought, that it must have paralysed him, because he moved not an inch from Delhi. Instead it was his daughter, Indira, who was tasked to go see to the good people of Jabalpur, but not before the roads she would take had been retarred. The stains of blood and burnt flesh had defeated the simple solution of soap and water that the municipal department had decided to employ at first. So it was decided that a layer of bitumen was necessary to shield the eyes of the prime minister's daughter from the blood of Indian citizens. She was the country's information minister, and I've always wondered what information she gathered for her shamed father. She was nobody's fool. Of course nothing came of it.'

Ahmed Saeed slumped, exhausted, and glowered, his gaze focused out to the city, to the rest of the country that had turned out so treacherous.

'Didn't Shabbir sahib go to Delhi?' Khan Jamali asked.

Ahmed Saeed said nothing. Then, after a while, he nodded but refused to say anything more.

Nobody had much to say after that, and one by one they made their excuses and slunk away.

Shabbir sahib had gone, Rafiq learned later. Not immediately, but he had gone. He had only just retired from the High Court in Allahabad, and he decided to go on his own, a private citizen who had served his country with honesty, and his head held high, used to passing judgement. He left for Jabalpur accompanied only by Rustam, telling nobody about his plans. The next thing people knew, he was in Delhi.

It was whispered that he had taken a petition, with a list of the guilty officers and politicians. He believed in backing everything with proof, and he thought he had it.

Weeks passed and Shabbir sahib didn't return from

Delhi. It was a month and a half before Rustam was seen polishing the Buick again and a light came on in Shabbir sahib's study. But everyone who came to call on him was turned away. He was no longer receiving visitors.

It was after that day that Ahmed Saeed took over the management of Shabbir Manzil, though out of respect for his father he never used the main dining room except for family meals. But servants' mouths are not as easily shut as the doors of great houses, and the rumour made its way out of Shabbir Manzil that the two large black-and-white photographs that had hung on either side of the dining table, one of Shabbir sahib with a beaming Sarojini Naidu looking lovely despite the plainness of her features and the other of him shaking hands with an energetic-looking Nehru, had been removed. It seemed as if both poetry and politics were no longer welcome, at least not in Shabbir sahib's room and study, which he now rarely left.

Outside, however, neither topic could be so easily ignored. People scanned the papers, heard rumours, and spoke in whispers. Jabalpur was only the first of many such incidents. Maybe like other businesses hate too needs to advertise its wares with one big bash before the usual day-to-day transactions can truly begin. It took a little while, a couple of years or so, but then pigs were released into a congregation gathered for Friday prayers in one town; a squabble over loudspeakers led to a killing in another town. A dead cow was mourned by the killing of three men somewhere else, and soon a rash of riots and curfews pockmarked the country.

These were grim times, and the men at Shabbir Manzil spoke softly and urgently. Drinking tea, they discussed poetry. Rafiq did his best, and by the fourth month after his marriage, he managed to blurt out his first sher in public.

'Humaara haal kuchh aisa hai,' he began and, when nobody interrupted, he carried on:

Humaara haal kuchh aisa hai, jaise ek dhalti hui deewar hai
Ek jo sahara mila, kisi aur ke ghar ka kona nikla.

After a moment one of the men at the gathering asked tentatively, 'Firaq?' trying to guess the name of the poet who had written a couplet so appropriate to their times: 'My condition is like that of a collapsing wall/ The one support I found was the corner of somebody else's home.'

Rafiq blushed when Ahmed Saeed said, 'Arre, can't you see that it is our Rafiq who has composed these lines?' In the twilight, though, nobody could see the colour in his cheeks.

He was so pleased with himself that he wanted to tell Shaista as soon as he returned to the far wing of Shabbir Manzil that was now their home. Instead he waited until they had sat down to dinner and he had mustered the courage to risk the prospect of her disinterest. But before he could tell her, she said, 'I'm going to be a mother.'

Later, after the sex that left him so confused and alone, he noticed how she slept, with her right hand cradling her stomach that showed not even the hint of pregnancy, and he reached out to touch his child. But she moved then, restless in her sleep, and he snatched his hand back.

4

She glowed, her skin almost translucent, her fine bones standing out in relief on her face. The cruel summer added its own touch to her fragile beauty, darkening the skin under her eyes, so that they shone.

Though their rooms were light and airy, with windows set both high and low in the walls to let in what ventilation could be had, Shaista suffered through the long months of pregnancy, but only physically. She was never happier than in those months, stroking the rising bulge of her belly when the women came to visit, singing little songs of love for her son. She had already determined that her child would be male, and that he would be named Jamaal, after the father that had left her too early, had abandoned her to her fate, something her son would never do.

He was born in late September, bloody and shining with her love, after a labour that stretched out almost three quarters of the day, having begun early in the morning and continuing until sunset, exhausting two sets of nurses and terrifying the doctor. Shaista was too exhausted to do anything more than hold her child for a moment as he squalled his anger at having been evicted from his comfortable home inside her, raging at the new freedom into which he had been delivered, unprepared. She pressed him to her body in arms too weak to hold properly, her fingers not bending the way they should, but spasmodically, until a nurse took the baby from her.

'No,' she said, 'no.' But the protest had no real force and she fell asleep almost immediately.

The doctor took Rafiq aside and into his office after the congratulations. Unable to face the father, he focused his gaze on the thick tomes in his glass-covered bookcase that he hadn't opened in years. 'Mr Ansari, you are aware that the birth was difficult.'

Rafiq nodded and then, realizing that the doctor had not seen the gesture, said, 'Yes, Doctor sahib.'

'It was more than difficult,' the doctor said. 'You are a very lucky man. We were lucky to save both the baby and the mother. At two points I was sure we would lose at least one, if not both, of them.'

'Thank you, Doctor,' Rafiq said, rising from his chair to show his gratitude and deference. 'I'm . . .'

But Dr Anil Srivastava cut him off. 'No, no,' he began but heard the impatience in his voice and paused briefly before continuing. 'I'm sorry that I'm not being clear, it's just . . .' and then he cleared his throat and said quickly, 'Value your son. He may be the only child you have.'

'Sir?' Rafiq asked.

'It is unlikely that your wife will survive a second pregnancy, much less another such difficult childbirth.'

A look swept over Rafiq's face and was gone so quickly that the doctor thought he had imagined it. But for a second he could have sworn that Rafiq looked relieved.

It took months for Shaista to recover her full strength. For the first two weeks she was on complete bed rest. In contrast, little Jamaal was so robustly healthy it seemed almost ill-mannered of him.

It had been years since a baby had entered Shabbir Manzil and he was the centre of attention of the many women of the household. Ahmed Saeed, too, became part of the boy's fan club, returning to the playful child he himself had been. It was rumoured that even Shabbir sahib would sit back in his study, close his books, and shut his eyes so he could soak in the sound of a child's happy laughter. Nobody had actually seen this, or if anybody had, it would have been Rustam, and Rustam would never speak about his master's doings. Still, somehow the word made its way out that the master of Shabbir Manzil was pleased.

If there was one person left out of the whole thing, it was Rafiq. At first it was because of the women. They took both Shaista and Jamaal into their custody, drawing them deep into the inner recesses of Shabbir Manzil, deeper than any stranger would ever be allowed to enter, and Rafiq was, after all, a stranger. He might have married one of them, might even have provided the master of the house with a reason to smile in the butt end of his days, but he was still a stranger to the family. There was a hurdle of blood and bone that could not be set aside by a mere job, or a marriage, or even the fathering of a son. It was a decision made by the women, and communicated almost by suggestion. The inner rooms were their territory, and when they took his wife and son there, he knew better than to follow. He knew that he wasn't welcome, and that he never would be.

Even after the first weeks of seclusion, when his wife and son came back to him, he seemed to have no rights over them. Maybe he had been expecting too much, but a birth, the near deaths, should have changed something. They had certainly changed things for him. He was eager to have Shaista back. He realized how important she was for him, how he had lost everybody who was close to him in acquiring her, and yet he had discovered nothing of her. Maybe it is true that a man sees nothing except his own self until he has seen death. His wife's brush with mortality had reminded Rafiq of his own death, and he understood for the first time how truly alone he was.

He would be a better husband now. He would be the husband he should have been. That was what he vowed to himself. Maybe he was doing nothing different from what many men have done through history, not just in this mohalla, or this town, but across the world, becoming husbands only after they have first become fathers.

Except that Shaista was not interested. It was not that she rejected his advances, more that he never had the courage to attempt them, knowing that she would brush him aside, swatting him away like some troublesome fly.

He tried then to reach out to his son, but the child cried

in Rafiq's arms, terrified by this overcautious parent, and
Shaista gave him no second chances, repossessing Jamaal
as if Rafiq was no more than a passing stranger who had
offered to care for the child, had offered and failed. She
rarely allowed him to hold Jamaal, or even care for him,
keeping a strict watch over the baby and attending to his
every need.

It would have been easier to accept if he was only one
of many denied access to the child, but it seemed as if every
other person could claim Jamaal. Ahmed Saeed led the
chorus, renaming the child 'Jimmy', playing with his toes,
bouncing him on his ample lap. Even Rustam was allowed
to play with the little boy, bringing shiny little tinsel, and
producing children's toys from some secret location that
nobody knew about. It was only Rafiq who had to stand
aside, who could not claim his only child.

Day after day, week after week, month after month, he
watched his child grow, heard him speak his first faltering
words. He watched as Jamaal took his first steps, watched
him fall, and had learned by that time to stay his hand, to
control his breathing, not to cry out or say anything, just
observe, even if it was difficult, even if he did still clench
his fists sometimes, until the veins rose, thick and distinct
on the back of his thin hands.

So he turned again to the place where he could find some
release: the gatherings at Shabbir Manzil, where he would
be among poems and poets. But there was little enough to
be had. He had slowly consolidated his position as a poet
of some worth, and now Ahmed Saeed would speak for

him, without fail. Wisely Rafiq had earlier chosen not to compete with the real poets, those who had been in the trade for years, and would have dismissed his fumbling efforts with a haughty sniff. The serious poets of Moazzamabad, all three of them, were known more for their eccentricities than for any great felicity with words. Shaukat Mian's long, thick mane had reached such proportions that it dwarfed his head and shoulders, and had forced him to abandon travelling in a bus or car for fear of damaging his precious tresses. Khan Jamali was famous for his rages; it was almost as if the anger of a seven-foot man had been crammed into a five-foot body. His passage down a street was always accompanied by the teasing of children and the inevitable explosion of profanities that followed. Lal Sahib was the only Hindu among them, and also the only one who produced good verse with any regularity, but he had a particular fixation on pens. Maybe it had to do with his many years as a schoolteacher; he always had half a dozen pens lining his jackets, none of which he ever used. Instead he would always request the use of somebody else's pen and, if the lender was not careful, it would be gone, added surreptitiously to Lal Sahib's collection, which the wise men gathering at Shabbir Manzil estimated must have run into a few thousand.

Before Jamaal's birth Rafiq had never challenged the authority of these poets. In their company he would rarely offer any of his own poems, relying mainly on the remembered verses of the great masters—Ghalib, Mir, maybe an occasional reference to Daag Dehlvi, or Wali

Dakkani. This forced the poets to ask him instead, to solicit couplets from him, and he would always demur, saying he couldn't remember the exact words until somebody at the gathering would begin to say the couplet, and only then would Rafiq break in and complete it. There was, after all, such a thing as too much modesty; if his verses were going to be recited, only he had a right to speak them, making sure they were not garbled into meaningless rubbish.

But now Rafiq, excluded from what he thought was rightfully his, began to feel that in four years not a word of praise had come his way. Shaukat Mian only shook his head wonderingly at a man who had the temerity to recite poetry when he could not even grow his hair. Khan Jamali glared at him, regarding him with the same undiluted rage that he extended to the rest of the universe that had failed to recognize his genius. Even Lal Sahib, who might have shown some consideration for a fellow teacher, only listened to him owlishly through the scratched lenses of his old pair of glasses, and then asked to see Rafiq's newly acquired Wing Sung fountain pen.

In a fit of petulance Rafiq said that the pen had run out of ink.

It was a bitter defeat, not the only one, nor the most bitter. At the college he had found that although Ahmed Saeed's recommendation had secured his job, not everybody thought that an MA first class and a BEd that was almost first class were all that impressive especially when he was teaching geography, a subject that he had last studied in school. And especially not when the principal of the college had a nephew who would have been perfect for the post, or so the principal made clear at least once every few months.

His only consolation was in his job. His students liked him. Among them he could at least nurture talent, reward the deserving, punish the lazy. Many of them were only a few years younger than him, but he had the power to treat them as if they were his children. With them he could be strict, or indulgent, as his mood suited him, and there was nobody to stop him from doing so. With them he was in control.

He couldn't say that about any other place, certainly not his home. When Rafiq had told Shaista about the doctor's comments, she had ignored him. It had mattered little at first. Her health and the needs of the baby had precluded even the idea of sex for several months, but when one night she pressed against him, her back arching into his chest, one leg reaching back to open his, he felt the same old wave of desire and despair.

'The doctor . . .' he whispered, but it was in her ear, as he reached out for her, gripping her shoulders, so that he could turn her towards him. 'The doctor,' he said again, but never finished what he had to say.

And was it such a bad thing? What was he protesting? How many men in the mohalla would have cut off their right hand for the chance that their wives would take half as much pleasure in their marital bed as they did? And after the relentless trials of a day, didn't a man have the right to seek pleasure in the arms of his wife? A confidence, even a recklessness, overcame Rafiq and a certain savagery edged his lovemaking. He buried his anger at her denial of him, protested the way that she kept his son away from him, and if she rode him to her own path to pleasure, well, he was not going to deny himself his own share.

Except that this was only at night, only what he told himself in bed, when the blood clouded his mind and he held down her wrists, taking his pleasure as she took hers, alone. Afterwards, in the morning, the doctor's words would come back to him and he would lie in bed, awake, but unable to rise because of the fear resting in the hollow of his neck, choking him. Months passed, then a year, and another, and there was no indication that he was putting his wife's life in danger, but there was no relief, only a confusion that occasionally became a vague resentment, even a dull anger, for reasons he couldn't any longer understand. And the fear remained.

It was in the mosque, some three years after he became a father, that he finally broke his silence, though not loudly and certainly not honestly.

He had risen for the pre-dawn prayers, up even before the azaan intruded into the silence calling all good Muslims to prayer, to salvation, and exhorting them to wake up: 'Prayer is better than sleep.' Since sleep was hardly an option, Rafiq figured prayer might as well do.

But there is more than prayer at the mosque, more than a gathering mumbling their aspirations, their fears, their confessions, their desire for exaltation to an unseen God.

There are familiars as well, and one of them was, inevitably, the imam, Maulana Qayoom.

'Maulana sahib,' Rafiq said after the prayers, speaking before he quite realized what he was saying, or why. 'Maulana sahib, you have not come to my house; you have not met my son.'

The imam smiled genially. 'These things can always be remedied, Rafiq.'

It took only a few minutes to walk to the house, and in those short moments Rafiq felt how good it all was, how perfect his plan. He burst into the house to tell the sleepy Shaista, 'Maulana sahib is here ... to see Jamaal.'

Of course she could not resist and, although the child was still half-asleep, he was brought from his warm bed. The imam protested, he did not wish to disturb the child's sleep, but the protests were half-hearted, and Jamaal was not at all troubled, his sleepy dreams giving way to include the sight of a man dressed in white sitting in the drawing room, with white hair and beard wreathing his face.

Jamaal reached to touch the beard, and the Maulana raised his right hand, his index finger held up. Jamaal clutched the bony finger.

'*Bolo Allah ek hai, Jamaal*,' the Maulana said playfully. *Say that God is one*. With the finger in his hand, Jamaal did not know what to say. He liked the genial face of the Maulana and his soft voice, but he was not used to this.

He looked around, searching for his mother, but Shaista was in the kitchen making tea. Instead it was Rafiq who said, '*Bolo, beta*.'

With only the questionable authority of his father to guide him, Jamaal dropped his eyes to the floor and mumbled, '*Allah ek hai*,' while slowly letting go of the Maulana's hand.

But the imam grabbed the young boy's finger again, holding it softly and asking, 'What did you say?'

It could have been a threat, but spoken so softly, and with a gentle smile, it became a game. And Jamaal knew all about games.

'*Allah ek hai*,' he said, in a stronger voice, and when Rafiq laughed softly, appreciatively, Jamaal started saying it repeatedly, excitedly, exclaiming '*Allah ek hai! Allah ek hai!*' as he danced around the room, his hand free now, but his right index finger held up triumphantly, pointing to the roof, and the unseen heavens beyond.

Shaista looked in from the doorway and, noticing an odd confederacy between the men, caught Rafiq's eye and gestured him to come to the kitchen. He would serve tea to the Maulana, as she excused herself from their company.

After that Rafiq became more regular with his pre-dawn prayers. Not that the Maulana came home every time afterwards, but once every few weeks Rafiq would invite him over, winning some time with his son.

It was odd, but it appeared to him—he allowed himself to believe—that after this Shaista began to address him differently. As if by playing, and winning, a difficult hand in the game between them, he had finally gained some respect. It was not deference, but his existence seemed to have taken some shape, and she had made a little space for it in her life.

In the pleasure of this contentment Rafiq lost sight of the things he needed to speak to Shaista about, or maybe it had become even more impossible.

It was natural, through this, for Rafiq to think that prayer would give him resolve. But at the morning prayers he found none within himself. Till one day, under the gathering storm of the politics afflicting the country, he thought he found some answers, but also other reasons to do nothing.

There was a group of young men speaking to the imam before the prayers began, and afterwards, they moved to intercept some of the faithful as they made to leave. Rafiq easily recognized some of the men who, like him, stopped to join the group: Rahmatullah sahib, Javed Habib, Mohsin Ahmed, Waris Abidi. They were all teachers. It was Maulana Qayoom who began the discussion.

'You are all familiar with the Emergency?' the imam asked in his soft voice.

It was a ridiculous question, and Javed almost laughed. 'Maulana sahib, we do live in the world, how could we be unaware of the Emergency? The whole of the country is under the rule of Mrs Gandhi's Congress and the leaders of all the rest of the political parties are being put in jail.'

'A good thing, too,' Mohsin said. 'What this country needs is development and not demonstrations.'

One of the serious young men flanking the Maulana cut in: 'You have no idea of what you are talking about.'

'What do you mean?' Mohsin bridled. The man was at least a decade younger than Mohsin, and sounded like he was from out of town. 'Who are these people, Maulana sahib?'

Maulana Qayoom had also been ruffled by the sharp intervention, but he only said, 'These are some friends from Delhi. Do listen.' But he still gave the young man a severe look.

'The woman has gone insane,' the young man said. He had moderated his tone, but anger burned in his eyes.

'Softly, Ahmed,' one of the other men cautioned, the only one with a beard among them, although it was clearly a recent addition to his face. He put a hand on the angry young man's shoulder, and turned to address Rafiq and the rest of the people from the mohalla. 'You'll have to forgive his anger. Ahmed believes strongly, but it is a difficult subject.'

Taking a deep breath, he asked, 'You have heard of the nasbandi programme?'

And this time nobody answered, although one or two of them shifted uneasily. The government's vasectomy initiative was not a comfortable topic of discussion.

'I presume you have,' the man continued. 'Well, under the Emergency the government is pushing it through by all means. Since there is strict censorship and because all the opposition politicians are in jail, there is little news of it, and nobody to raise the issue.'

'What does it matter?' Mohsin asked. He was still angry at the way he had been addressed. 'If people want to get their tubes tied, what does it matter to us? It isn't as if India suffers from a lack of children.'

'It is forbidden, that is why it matters,' Ahmed cut in heatedly. 'It is *haraam*. Haraam. It is God, and God alone, who determines who is to be born and who is to die.'

Mohsin made to rise. 'I think it's time for me to go.'

Again it was Maulana Qayoom who intervened. 'Please, Mohsin sahib, please stay. This is important.'

Nobody had heard the imam ask for anything before, and maybe it was just the surprise that made them pay attention.

The bearded man sighed and said, 'I'm sorry, this is a matter of strong emotion. My name is Qamruddin, and I used to be an anaesthesiologist at a hospital in Ghaziabad, just outside Delhi. A month ago I was told that we were to perform a heavy load of operations over the next few days. We performed twenty vasectomies the first day, and it was only afterwards, when I was going through the paperwork, that I realized all the men were Muslim. When I went to the recovery ward to talk to them, not one of them knew about the operation that had been performed on them. They had just been picked up by the District Magistrate and carted over for a "check up". When I confronted the doctor, he told me that the order had come from the government. All officials are being assigned a quota—they have to ensure a fixed number of nasbandis are performed in the areas under their supervision.'

Qamruddin added, 'It is the poor that are being targeted, the poor and Muslims. Who will speak up for them? When I complained to the doctor he said we had a surplus of poor people and Muslims in India. This would take care of poverty and Muslims in one go. That was before he remembered that I was a Muslim as well.'

There was a fraught silence, until one of the men from the mohalla said, 'Maybe it will all blow over. We haven't received any reports here.'

'You will,' Qamruddin answered heavily, 'you will. And then you'll have to decide what to do.'

Maulana Qayoom spoke now. 'Many of you are government employed. If it comes to a choice between your salary and standing by the people of your faith, I hope God will show you a way.'

The discussion continued for a while, but one by one everybody left, suitably serious. Qamruddin, Ahmed and the two other men with them left as well to catch the faithful at another mosque. It was then that Rafiq asked Maulana Qayoom, 'Is contraception haraam, Maulana sahib?'

The maulana cocked his head and thought before he replied. 'In this case, definitely. Not just because it is being done by deceit and force, but also because the idea behind it is false. It is God that provides for people. The richest often destroy their wealth, or a calamity takes it away from them; only God can give to the poorest, and guide them to salvation. It isn't our right to halt a life for that. We must trust in God, submit to His Will, that is Islam.'

'So it is haraam?' Rafiq persisted.

'Not in all cases,' the Maulana replied. 'Not if it endangers the mother's life, or something like that.'

And Rafiq wanted to say something then, something

about Shaista, he wanted to ask for help, but Maulana Qayoom was now asking him a question: 'And you, what will you do? The Alvi College receives government funding.'

'I will act as a Muslim,' Rafiq mumbled, and rose to flee, knowing that he wouldn't. That he wouldn't have the strength to tell Shaista what the Maulana had said. Even religion did not give him the courage to face her and tell her that nothing justified her insistence on having another child, not at the risk of her own death. Islam disapproved.

As for that other thing, the nasbandi programme, Rafiq became principled through no fault of his own. When the government announced that teachers' salaries would only be given when they had met their 'quota', when they had ensured that the required number of men submitted to the scalpel, there was genuine outrage, and there was a stand-off. The government cut off funding to the Alvi College, and the teachers' union decided to take a voluntary pay cut proportional to the amount of funding. Some donors pooled in a little more money, and the college managed to limp along. Other measures of the Emergency too moved forward, but haltingly, and by the time they touched Moazzamabad most of their force had been spent.

In either case Mrs Gandhi and her travails were of no real concern to Rafiq; he had troubles of his own. Three months before Jamaal was to turn five, Shaista became pregnant once again.

Dr Srivastava took a moment to remember them, and then immediately lost his temper. 'Are you mad?' he said to Rafiq. 'Do you know that she almost died last time?'

Rafiq had to swallow his anger before he could speak. 'It has been five years.'

'Please,' Dr Srivastava snapped. 'I know how long it has been. This is in my own handwriting,' he said, pointing at the file he had open on his desk.

After a moment the doctor spoke again, wearily this time, in defeat. 'You'll have to think of aborting the baby.'

'No,' Shaista said.

'Ma'am,' Dr Srivastava began, trying to reason with her, but Shaista wouldn't let him.

'No,' she said. 'No one is going to kill my baby.' And she rose to leave, pulling Rafiq along in her wake.

Two days later Ahmed Saeed dropped in to their wing of Shabbir Manzil. Jamaal answered the door, and immediately hugged one of Ahmed Saeed's legs. 'Toffee, toffee,' he cried.

'What do we have here?' Ahmed Saeed asked gravely. 'Am I being held for ransom, and that too by Jimmy the pirate, the companion of Brave Sindbad of the wild seas?'

Jamaal, who didn't know the word ransom, but did know Sindbad and, more importantly, knew that Ahmed Saeed never went anywhere without a sweet on his person, nodded vigorously.

Ahmed Saeed fumbled in one pocket, and then another, until one hand emerged holding the distinct orange, brown and gold wrapping of Jamaal's favourite chocolate toffee. Patting the delighted child on his head, Ahmed Saeed said, 'Now go tell your parents that your Bade-abbu is here.'

Rafiq was already there, extending his hand. 'As salaam aleikum, Ahmed Saeed sahib,' he said. 'You'll have tea?'

'Wa aliekum as salaam, Rafiq,' Ahmed Saeed replied, and nodded.

Shaista got the tea ready, and brought out a box of biscuits that Ahmed Saeed refused to touch at first, but he took one after much coaxing. Satisfied, Shaista left to run after her son.

'Rafiq,' Ahmed Saeed said when they were alone, 'Anil tells me that Shaista is expecting again?'

And when Rafiq didn't reply, Ahmed Saeed explained that he meant Anil Srivastava, the doctor. 'I've known Anil since my schooldays; he was a year senior to me. Bright chap. We always knew he'd do well.' Then, interrupting the hearty confidence, he added, 'I met him last night at the club and he mentioned that he was worried.'

'Contraception is forbidden in Islam. It is forbidden, haraam,' Rafiq said, the words coming out hard and angry, in the tone that the young man from Delhi, Ahmed, had used a year ago. He hadn't expected to say it, but now in his agitation, this was what came out. Mumbling, he added, 'It is our responsibility to multiply according to God's command.'

Ahmed Saeed was so nonplussed that he nearly dropped his half-eaten biscuit. He had never imagined hearing something like this from Rafiq.

As Ahmed Saeed floundered for a response, Rafiq rose from his chair and picked up the newspaper. Bringing it back to the table, he opened it to the second page and pointed to the top right-hand corner of the page. 'Riot in Fatehgarh,' he read out. 'Three dead.' Pointing to an article on the facing page he read, 'Meerut, 14 injured.'

Unwilling to stop lest the trembling of his lips became apparent to Ahmed Saeed, he said, 'Nobody seems to care when a Muslim dies, but one more Muslim child and the world will come to an end! That is what happened with the nasbandi programme, that's what it was all about although everyone pretends it was about something else. A plot to make sure that there are no more Muslims, no more children among us, that's what it was.'

Ahmed Saeed struggled to respond. 'The nasbandi programme wasn't aimed at Muslims,' he said, 'and however stupid it was, it has been brought to a halt.'

Rafiq took a moment to respond, gathering courage from a weird place, from the conversation after those pre-dawn prayers, the ones that Ahmed Saeed never attended, and so had never heard the men from Delhi and their stories. 'The nasbandi programme might not have been aimed at Muslims, but it hit them, all right,' Rafiq said quietly and surely now. It wasn't a tone he had used before, certainly not with Ahmed Saeed. He looked up and asked, 'Ahmed Saeed sahib, aren't you the one who told us about Jabalpur?'

'What on earth does *that* have to do with all this?' Ahmed Saeed said, half in irritation, half in panic at a conversation he had lost all control of. 'Anil is a doctor. This is a doctor's duty.'

'And no doubt all those vasectomies were the work of dutiful doctors,' Rafiq countered, completely addled now in the force of his words. Unable to contain himself, he rose and started to pace across the room, a dark energy animating his gestures. 'I will tell you what will happen, Ahmed Saeed sahib, I'll tell you what one more child will mean,' he said, his voice shaking. 'If it's a girl, Jamaal will have a sister to guard and protect, and if it's a boy, he will have a brother to watch his back, at least one person to trust in this world.'

What he didn't say was that if there was another child, he might have the chance to spend time with his own son—his exile and humiliation might end. Instead he spoke of God, and said, 'What is forbidden is forbidden for a purpose, Ahmed Saeed sahib.'

'If that's what you want,' Ahmed Saeed said, rising in irritation.

'It isn't what we want that matters,' Rafiq said. 'It is God's command, and we must obey. We must submit to His Will. That is Islam.'

5

Shaista had never heard Rafiq's anger. She did not think he had it in him, this thin cipher that her brother had handed her over to, this man whose life revolved around the non-existent praise of neighbourhood poets and a job that had come to him as a dowry.

She had stopped to take a breath while Jamaal scampered around the courtyard, laughing in that carefree way that caught in her throat, when she heard Rafiq's raised voice. It had taken her a moment to reach close enough to hear him say, 'If it's a girl, Jamaal will have a sister to guard and protect, and if it's a boy, he will have a brother to watch his back, at least one person to trust in this world.'

Such simple words, and spoken with no great flair for oratory, just a tight anger, and yet they meant so much to her, bringing sudden tears to her eyes. And with those tears something eased in her and she looked again at Rafiq, at the husband she had never seen.

It was a strange love, one that came so late and in a woman who had long ago lost any thought or hope of any, and had never expected to love this man, of all people. But maybe all love is a misunderstanding of a kind.

Shaista held him that night, after Jamaal had slipped off to sleep, held his face before the lovemaking, kissing him gently, and held him afterwards, wrapping herself around him, keeping him safe, treasuring him. Perhaps Rafiq should have asked her why, perhaps he could have spoken to her about the danger of her pregnancy and saved her. With her newfound love for him maybe she wouldn't have been so desperate for another child. But he had never had the courage to speak to her before, when she had not loved him. Now, when he was loved, how could he be suddenly brave with all this to lose? He took the coward's way out, and was merely grateful, not questioning at all. And who among us can blame him for that? How many men have been brave in the face of love, especially when they suspect that they are undeserving of it? And if there really are such men, certainly there were few of them in the town of Moazzamabad, in the mohalla of Rasoolpur. Here courage was conspicuous by its absence. Nobody ever spoke openly about anything; all the accusations were by insinuation; every blow was a stab in the back.

The day after that confrontation with Ahmed Saeed, Rafiq found himself again at the gathering of poets. Of course Ahmed Saeed was there and Rafiq wanted to apologize. He meant to, and he truly was sorry, but there was more to him now, a happiness that he could not hide. Ahmed Saeed was quick to notice that Rafiq's distraction was not that of a penitent, but that of a self-absorbed lover. He had no need for the favours of Shabbir Manzil at that moment. Shaista had given him a sense of entitlement.

With an effort, Ahmed Saeed controlled the anger that flared up at this realization. Instead, he turned to poetry to mock Rafiq. 'What was that sher of Akbar Allahabadi's?' he asked the gathering. 'Something about the mullah declaring that the train was passé, hadn't Islam given us the camel?'

There was a shifting of seats as people tried to recall the verse, but despite two or three attempts nobody could.

Rafiq asked, stupidly, 'Are you sure it was Akbar's?'

And to that Ahmed Saeed released the full pent-up force of his anger. 'Of course I'm sure!' he all but shouted. 'Who else could put the religious fools in their place better than Akbar?'

Everyone sat still, and noted the anger on Ahmed Saeed's face, the bafflement and guilt on Rafiq's, and they understood that things had changed.

Lal Sahib started polishing his scratched glasses, and said in a quiet, measured voice, 'Yes, Akbar had a lovely touch. I don't recall the sher you mean, Ahmed Saeed sahib, but there was that other one of his:

> '*Beparda kal jo nazar aaieen chand beebian,*
> *Akbar zamin mein ghairate Qaumi se garh gaya;*
> *Poochha jo unse aap ka parda woh kya hua*
> *Kahne lagin ke aql pe mardon ki parh gaya.*'

(Yesterday, when I saw some unveiled ladies,

Akbar was swallowed up by the earth in shame for his community;

When I asked them where their veil had gone,

They replied that it had covered the minds of men.)

'A lovely one to remember, Lal Sahib,' Shaukat Mian said in appreciation.

Even Ahmed Saeed nodded. 'Not the one I was searching for, but a beautiful one. These silly religious types talk in terms of veils and shame when it is their own minds that are blinded.' He paused, then said, 'And it is always the women that suffer.'

This time the silence that settled on the group was both deep and embarrassed. This was a gathering of men; where did women figure in their conversation? And as if to change the subject, Khan Jamali, noticing the shadow of a stubble on Rafiq's chin, growled, 'Arre Rafiq, are you trying to grow a beard? You're not becoming a mullah, are you?'

'Yes, watch out for them,' Shaukat Mian chimed in, 'you know what Faiz Ahmed Faiz said: *Shaikh sahib se rasm o raah na ki/ Shukr hai zindagi kharaab na ki* (I didn't spend time discussing tradition with the Sheikh/ Thank goodness I didn't ruin my life).'

Ahmed Saeed snorted with laughter at that, and it caught on, with the rest joining in. All except Rafiq. He felt the blood rise in his face, but there was nothing he could say. Till the azaan saved him. Or trapped him. As the loudspeaker crackled into life in the mosque only a few dozen yards away, Rafiq sprang to attention.

'I'll be going,' he said. 'It's time for the maghrib prayers.'

That silenced them. For all their mockery of the mullahs and sheikhs, and whatever they might have said about religion, none of them could say a word that would stop a man from going to the mosque. And then, foolishly, Rafiq went one step too far. As he exited the patio, he bowed exaggeratedly to Lal Sahib and said with unnecessary emphasis, 'As salaam aleikum.'

At another time it might have meant nothing. After all, what do the words mean except a wish for peace upon the receiver. It was merely a greeting. But it was also a Muslim greeting, spoken too deliberately by a Muslim to a Hindu, the only Hindu among them who made his way every day to this neighbourhood dominated by Muslims because of his love of poetry, to this house of high culture and refinement where he had always been treated only as another poet.

As Lal Sahib fumbled to respond, Ahmed Saeed leapt up in his defence. 'You forget your place, Rafiq!'

'I can't even wish peace to one of your guests, Ahmed Saeed sahib?' Rafiq asked in false surprise.

That response sent Ahmed Saeed into a fury, his face turning purple. 'Out!' he yelled, one quivering finger pointed to the gate.

'From your house to God's,' Rafiq answered, and bowed.

His behaviour was amazing, more amazing to himself than to anybody else. His head spun with what he had just said and done, the sarcasm in his voice with which he had addressed Ahmed Saeed. What was the matter with him? Had he gone insane?

And then the fear hit him.

He was nothing without the favour of Shabbir Manzil, his job, his marriage, even his house, were in the hands of the person he had so gratuitously insulted. And for what? He could not tell.

At the mosque the ritual of ablution brought him some calm as he splashed the water on his face, over his arms and his feet. The prayers were soothing as well, and he stood, then bowed, and straightened only to genuflect again in the company of the fifty or so faithful gathered in the courtyard.

But maghrib prayers are short, and soon he had nothing left to do. Usually he would sit at the gathering of poets till quite late, getting up just in time to make his way home for dinner. Now he had nowhere to go.

So he went home.

Shaista was surprised to see him back so early. She had a knife in her hands, with a potato half cut. Jamaal clung to her shalwar and looked up at his father's unfamiliar face, contorted with some fierce emotion.

'I decided to come home after the namaaz,' Rafiq explained, his words hurried and slightly ashamed, and Shaista understood something of what had happened. It could only have been some insult at the hands of Ahmed Saeed, and she burned with his humiliation. Turning away quickly so that he would not see the anger in her eyes, she said, 'I have been teaching Jamaal the numbers. Will you do that so that he doesn't bother me in the kitchen?'

And so it was that father and son sat down together for the first time in the drawing room and Rafiq addressed the boy solemnly, 'As salaam aleikum, Jamaal.'

Jamaal only watched him, solemn-faced, until Shaista

who could hear everything through the open door to the kitchen, said, 'Answer your father, Jamaal.'

'As salaam aleikum, Baba.'

Sweat broke out on Rafiq's scalp, and he found he could not speak to his son. So he called out to Shaista, 'How much does he know?'

'I can count up to ten,' Jamaal said, and Rafiq's heart felt as if it would pound its way out of his chest for sheer pride.

'Mamujaan,' Jamaal said, meaning Ahmed Saeed, 'gave me a Cadbury's éclair the first time I counted up to ten.'

'Your father will give you two éclairs,' Shaista said promptly.

'*Sach?*' Jamaal asked in excitement.

'*Sach*,' Rafiq promised.

Of course poor Jamaal got it wrong, remembering only up to six and then jumping straight to nine, and Rafiq, who had so desperately wanted to buy his son one toffee more than Ahmad Saeed, could not hide his disappointment. Jamaal stood up and ran to his mother for shelter.

'Ammi, Ammi!' he demanded. 'Second chance. Please ask Baba to give me a second chance.'

Rafiq followed his son to the kitchen, but did not step in. This was Shaista's domain and although Jamaal could barge in, Rafiq could not.

'Uffo,' Shaista exclaimed, 'you'll make me cut my fingers, Jamaal,' but she was laughing.

'Of course you can have a second chance,' Rafiq said, and looking up at his wife, her eyes alive with joy, he added, 'everyone deserves a second chance.'

It was a lie. He knew that, as foolish, as vain and as small as he was, there were things he could never return to. His reputation at the gatherings in Shabbir Manzil had been decimated, partially out of his own pettiness. He felt ashamed now for putting Lal Sahib in such a spot and realized that he would rather have *his* forgiveness than Ahmed Saeed's. But that chance too was gone. Still, he could ignore all that for the present, could laugh with his wife, take pleasure in their son. They could eat together at the dinner table, and when Shaista started to clear up the table she said to him, 'Why don't you take Munna to the mosque? He's old enough to keep quiet even if he's too young to pray.'

That was their first excursion together, as father and son, Rafiq holding his son's hand far more tentatively than Jamaal clutched his. Along the way Rafiq stopped at a corner shop and bought his son not two but three Cadbury éclairs, making the excited child promise to eat them only when the prayers were done.

The night prayers are the longest, reflecting the old desert habits when the Arabs had time, and finally the cool, to remember God. Jamaal was not the only child present at the mosque, a few others had accompanied their parents, but they started to play and scuffle in the back rows. Occasionally, between breaks, one of the elders would turn around and glare, silencing the children for a few moments. But they knew that the adults would have to go back to the prayers and they could resume their games. And anyway, they were safe from the wrath of their parents. Men feared the wrath of God enough here not to raise their hands in anger.

Jamaal sat through all this quietly in the corner, clutching the éclairs in his fist. After the last set of prayers, Rafiq turned and saw his son sprawled asleep. As the others of the congregation left, Rafiq rose to say one final short prayer, of thanksgiving.

6

Something happened after that, a miracle perhaps, or maybe Fate just forgot about Shaista and Rafiq for some time.

Shaista's second pregnancy was as trouble-free as the first had been difficult. And though she glowed once again, there were no shadows under her eyes. Even in the seventh month of her pregnancy, when the child had ballooned her belly and his kicks could be felt even by curious little Jamaal, Shaista moved with a grace that wasn't of this base and broken world. She was sure it would be a boy again, and she had decided to name the child Mahfooz, the one who is safe, because she knew that both her husband and her eldest son would take care of the new child. She knew how much that meant, knew how necessary it was, hadn't she seen it in her own life? And now she was seeing it again as Shabbir Manzil closed its heart to her husband.

Rafiq spent more time at home now. He had so few places to go to. The college was his only outlet, but after teaching he could not spend his time there: besides, the taint of his fall in social status meant that the other teachers didn't want to be associated with him. The principal had become more obnoxious and Rafiq found that after his bout with Ahmed Saeed he had little courage to take on another fight.

Instead he began spending more time at home with his son, whom he suddenly had so much access to. And if he had lost one audience for his poetry, he gained another with Shaista who, after the fourth month of her pregnancy, had taken leave from teaching and spent time at home, reading and sleeping. He had started tentatively, quoting a few verses to her from the book she was reading, and when she replied with a few by another poet, Rafiq had slyly inserted a verse of his own.

She was delighted, and surprised. In all their time together she had had no idea of what actually happened at the afternoon gatherings at Shabbir Manzil. She had been dismissive of it, considering it little more than the useless gossip of idle, middle-aged men, and she had been partially repulsed because Rafiq had so desired those gatherings. But now as he recited to her the verses he had composed, she felt a thrill of unexpected intimacy. She tried to match him, quoting the poets she remembered, and clumsily trying to shape poetry of her own. In truth what she was doing was remembering bits and pieces she had written many years ago, when she wanted to capture the feel of poverty, but with dignity. She had not succeeded, and she had put those thoughts away, but now she tried to recall them, speaking them for the first time ever to another human being.

Her verses were not as polished as his, but at times there would be a line of such striking insight that he would exclaim in delight. It was at such moments that he missed acutely the company of other poets, even the stern Khan Jamali and the owlish Lal Sahib.

Unused to her approval, and in his gratitude for what she now gave him—something approaching love—he responded with devotion, which would have appeared clumsy had it not been so reckless. If only she were a man! It was *her* place, not his, to have sat there in that gathering, and she would have acquitted herself better than he had.

'Don't say that,' Shaista replied when he spoke his thoughts. She put her hand on his mouth to emphasize the point. 'Don't say that. You stood up for me, you spoke for me. What man could acquit himself better?'

And then he longed to tell her the truth, but it was so complicated and he was so scared that all he could say was, 'You don't understand.'

His misery made her all the more committed to stand by him in his hour of need; so when the women of Shabbir Manzil came to call on her now and invite her into the inner courtyards of that grand house, she always refused. She would not enter the inner sanctum of a family that had insulted her husband. And even when Rafiq stepped out of the house, Shaista insisted that he take little Jamaal along.

There was, in any case, only one real place that the father and son could go to, and that was the mosque. It was Rafiq's time alone with his son, so the visits became frequent. And somehow, because these things follow their own secret logic, Rafiq started to grow a beard, making true the mockery that Khan Jamali had flung his way. It gave his thin face a look of strength that had been missing, and he found that the students paid greater attention to him in class, especially if he also frowned once in a while.

Meanwhile, Fate, or whoever had been on duty, remembered Shaista in her eighth month, and she collapsed into a faint in the middle of a sentence. Luckily she had been leaning against Rafiq when it happened so he could catch her as her body lurched suddenly forward.

'Mumma!' Jamaal yelled, but for once Rafiq had no time for his son. As the child scrambled around the scene, scared as much by his father's uncharacteristic silence as by Shaista's, Rafiq lifted his wife in his arms, amazed by how light she was even with child, and carried her to the bedroom. When he had set her down, he sat next to her and held her wrist and felt her pulse running at a rate that terrified him. She had been radiating heat when he carried her, but he was still surprised by how her forehead burned with fever under the palm of his hand.

'Jamaal,' he said, finally turning to his bewildered son, 'watch your mother for a few minutes. I'm going to fetch a rickshaw.'

Fifteen minutes later father and son were at the hospital, accompanying the still unconscious Shaista. It was another half hour before Dr Srivastava finally sat down and spoke to Rafiq. He was too tired for anger, but some of it still seeped through. 'There's something wrong with the baby. The blood supply is choked, and we'll have to perform a

Caesarean immediately. I doubt we can save the child. We may just be able to save your wife.'

What he didn't say was that it was all Rafiq's fault, but he was so disgusted with the man sitting across the table that he didn't even look him in the face.

The baby was dead long before they managed to cut it out of its mother's womb. It had been a girl.

It took Shaista eighteen hours to recover consciousness. With nobody to turn to, Rafiq had deposited Jamaal at his own parents' home, the first time they had their grandson to themselves. When Rafiq had turned to leave, having ended his exile from his parents' life as abruptly as he had chosen it, his father stopped him at the door.

'Do you want me to come with you?'

Out of pride, Rafiq had shaken his head, though he had waited a little at the door, taking a while to pull on his shoes. But his father hadn't repeated the offer.

Rafiq was asleep on the hard metal bench next to Shaista's bed when she woke up in the middle of the night. Feeling the pain in her stomach, she reached out to feel her suddenly flattened belly, and running her hands over the stitches she started weeping. She didn't need anybody to tell her what had happened. Her sobs were too soft to wake Rafiq, but then, as she tried to sit up, the intravenous cord caught on one of the bottles by her bedside and it exploded on the floor in a spray of shattered glass and pills.

Rafiq jumped awake, and put a foot down on the floor before he realized what had happened. But he was lucky, and only one small shard cut into his heel before the stab of pain stopped him. He reached down with his right hand and felt across the sole of his foot until he felt the edge of the shard, and pulled it out as he said softly, 'Gently, Shaista, gently, you're all right now.' But that made her weep all the harder.

In the dim glow of the night lamp Rafiq located his sandals, and then made his way to her bedside. He had just put his hand around her head, cradling her, when the nurse arrived. Rafiq said nothing, nor looked up at her. The nurse didn't need directions; she had seen the aftermath of many tragedies, and a broken bottle of pills was a small matter. It took her only moments to clean up, then she left the grieving couple to each other's ministrations.

'Where is Jamaal?' Shaista asked finally.

'With my family,' Rafiq answered.

'I so wanted him to have a brother . . .'

'There will be other chances,' he said, although he knew there wouldn't, not for Shaista. The damage that the dead child had done to her was immense, the doctor had told him. She would be lucky to survive.

'I wanted this one,' she said, and there was no answer to that. He could only hold her as she wept herself to exhaustion.

As she slipped into sleep she said to him, commanded him, 'Stay with me.'

'Always.'

But he wasn't there when she awoke. There was only her brother, and Ahmad Saeed.

'Where is Rafiq?' she asked.

'Outside,' Ahmad Saeed said. As tired as she was, his tone enraged her. She knew that her husband would have been here if not for these two, knew that he would have been true to his word if not for them and their undue power. They had already humiliated him because he had spoken for her, and now they had made him break his promise to her. How much more would they do to break him?

Maybe that was why her look was so withering when she turned to the man who had been her caretaker all her life, and asked, 'Why are you here?'

'Bitiya,' he said, flabbergasted, 'how could I not come?'

'I have somebody to take care of me,' she said. 'You married me off to him.'

'And I am so sorry, Bitiya,' Ismat Sharif cried. 'Forgive me. Had I known that this is what he would do to you, I would never have approved of the marriage!'

'Anil, the doctor, he warned that rascal Rafiq. And even I tried,' Ahmad Saeed said. 'We are sorry.'

'It was *my* son,' Shaista said fiercely.

They went blank for a moment, and then Ismat said, 'It was a girl.'

She would have hit them for that, if not for all the other things they had done. She would have struck them for not understanding that the baby had been her choice, her desire, and that the man they were maligning had been her partner in it, a willing one. If there had been a crime, it was she who was the criminal. He had become an accomplice only out of loyalty. Out of love.

'Bitiya,' Ismat said again, 'I had no idea of the type of man he was.'

'He seemed all right,' Ahmad Saeed added, 'educated and well spoken. But maybe he was just after the land.'

'What?' she asked.

'You know he comes from a common family, and maybe he thought he would inherit the land.'

'What land?' she asked again, confused.

Ismat fidgeted, and Ahmad Saeed asked, 'She doesn't know?'

Ismat looked at him, then at his sister, and then back at Ahmad Saeed. 'There was never a time to tell her.' He turned to Shaista, looking like a man confused by a sudden turn a conversation has taken. 'Bitiya, it never occurred to me to tell you, it was not important. You know the law. No one person can own more than twelve and a half acres of farmland. So in his will father left ten acres in your name.'

He hesitated, and continued, 'And you know that is the law under Shariah. Daughters inherit a third, and sons, two-thirds.'

She closed her eyes then, to keep back the tears.

'Bitiya?'

'What about Jamaal?' she asked without opening her eyes.

'Precisely,' Ismat said, 'we thought Rafiq would use your son to lay claim to my land.'

'You have the papers?' she asked, scared now that her voice would give her away, that she would cry again and

Ismat would reach out to comfort her when her skin crawled at the thought of his touch.

There was a pause, and there was strain in Ismat's voice when he answered, 'I had a lawyer draw them up.'

She opened her eyes, the anger burying her need to cry. 'Give them to me.'

She signed them, quickly, clumsily, her handwriting legible despite the tubes and weakness. She signed away a birthright she had never known about, putting it in the name of Ismat's wife. It was only when she was done that she spoke. 'Send Rafiq in.'

'Are you sure?' Ismat asked.

She let all her contempt and pain colour her reply. 'He never came to me with any papers, Bhaijaan.'

Ismat started, and she knew that he did love her, that it was not a lack of love that had destroyed what they had, but fear. Something had broken him in that long slide to a state of near poverty. Those long, hard years had depleted him, made him so much smaller than he should have been.

But she had no time for all that. She had no time to attempt forgiveness. She didn't care.

'Please,' she said. 'Please, just leave.'

Rafiq rushed in as soon as they had left, and found her weeping. Gently he reached his hands around the tubes and pulled her head as close to him as possible.

She put out her free arm and wrapped it around his waist, her head resting on his stomach. She could feel his heart thumping away from there, a little faster than normal, but steady, secure.

'Don't ever leave me again.'

'Never,' he promised. 'Never.'

She died two hours later, her hand going limp in his grip as she slept. He called out for a nurse. They responded quickly, rushing to rescue her, but she was gone. One of the doctors started pounding on her chest to revive her, using all his strength as he brought down his fist hard, and that was too much for Rafiq.

'Stop!' he shouted. 'Stop. Just let her be.'

7

Shabbir Manzil acted quickly in the wake of Shaista's death; quickly but not rashly. The first emissary was Ahmad Saeed, seeking rapprochement, or so it seemed. At her grave after the soil had been thrown in by her relatives, and then by all those who had come through ties of community, Ahmad Saeed said to Rafiq, 'Where's Jimmy?'

Rafiq took a moment to respond. He had forgotten the peculiar nickname; Ahmad Saeed had been conspicuous by his absence over the last few months.

'He's with my mother,' Rafiq said. 'There was no point in bringing him to the graveyard.'

Ahmad Saeed nodded, and then, after a few moments, said, 'He must miss his mother.'

Rafiq was silent at that. What was there to say?

Ahmad Saeed cleared his throat and finally came to the point. 'It would probably do Jimmy good if he spent time with his aunts in Shabbir Manzil. They'll take care of him.'

Rafiq was already nodding absentmindedly when Ahmad Saeed rounded off the proposal by saying, 'Anyway, they've seen so little of him since Shaista fell ill.'

It was stupid, and unnecessary, but maybe Ahmad Saeed felt the need to justify himself, or had just become garrulous for a lack of anything meaningful to say. But it reminded Rafiq of what had happened over the last few months. That the women of Shabbir Manzil had seen little of Jamaal of late was true, but it wasn't because Shaista was ill. Her health had deteriorated only at the end; long before that she had stopped visiting the other women of Shabbir Manzil, coldly furious at the way they were treating her husband. She forbade Jamaal from going as well, explaining to Rafiq, 'It's wrong to send a child into a house that doesn't respect his father. What can they teach him except disrespect for his own family?'

Rafiq had been uneasy about that, and had wanted to tell her the truth about his encounter with Ahmed Saeed, and maybe Jamaal could then have been the bridge to his reconciliation with Shabbir Manzil. That was what he had thought then. But now that Ahmad Saeed mentioned it, Rafiq felt a wave of revulsion rise up in his throat until it choked him. *Why did they have to lie? What was the point? And if they cared so much, why had they waited to ask till she was dead?*

Keeping his head bowed Rafiq said softly, 'He's all right where he is.'

His words were too soft for Ahmad Saeed, who leaned over to ask, 'What?'

'I said that Jamaal is all right where he is,' Rafiq repeated forcefully. 'My mother can teach him what he needs to know.'

Baffled, Ahmad Saeed could only ask, 'Are you sure?'

Rafiq raised his eyes, furious, and said, 'Yes.'

Three hours later when Rafiq arrived at Shabbir Manzil he found Rustam waiting for him. 'Where should I take you?' the servant asked.

'What?'

'You are no longer welcome in Shabbir Manzil,' Rustam said. 'Where shall I take you?'

Pushing the man aside Rafiq made his way into the house. Rustam recovered his balance and hurried after him. The door to what had been Rafiq's and Shaista's home stood open, and outside it were a stack of trunks and a few bundles tied together in bedsheets, like a dhobi's washload.

'What is this?' Rafiq asked.

'This is what I couldn't fit into the jeep. The rest of your belongings are there,' Rustam answered. And this time Rafiq didn't try to assert himself. He didn't even step inside the door. Instead he followed Rustam out of Shabbir Manzil, got into the jeep, and asked to be taken to his parents' house. But during the drive his skin began to crawl and itch, and he turned to Rustam and asked, 'Do you know where Ajmal Khan lives?'

'The principal of Alvi College?'

'Yes. Take me there.'

'Now?' Rustam asked, sounding impatient.

'Yes, *now*, before you drop me home.' Rafiq's voice was shrill, and he shut up before it cracked. He crossed his arms and hugged them to himself as the jeep made its way across town.

Ajmal Khan lived in the newly built Rudrapur colony. Moazzamabad's population had been expanding for decades, and old neighbourhoods like Rasoolpur had initially tried to cope by building on top of already existing structures, or by packing more people into already crowded rooms. But as new money appeared—with the owners of sugar factories, jewellery traders, cinema hall owners, and people who rented out their land as the railway lines running east from Delhi got busier—new colonies like Rudrapur were coming up. They were far from pretty, but at least they had covered drains, electricity poles and real roads, tarred and with two lanes, instead of the glorified alleys that criss-crossed the old parts of town.

And all the new colonies had Hindu names. They still do, as you would have noticed. Many more, in fact, than in the years I'm telling you about.

It was funny, but as the jeep wound its way out of the alleys of Rasoolpur, then Urdu Bazaar, into the main market of Narangi Chowk heading towards the railway station, and beyond the railway lines to Rudrapur, Rafiq was struck for the first time by the realization that Moazzamabad, despite its name gifted by a Mughal prince with more pomp than power, was a predominantly Hindu town. He had never thought about it before; in fact, he had never really thought about what was happening outside of Rasoolpur. Despite the supposedly learned discussions every evening at Shabbir Manzil, all that Rafiq knew about the wider world was from newspapers and gossip, maybe a little from the radio. He had never travelled very far from his mohalla, had never made friends with people from a different neighbourhood. The only time that he stepped out of Rasoolpur was when he went to teach at the college, and he was struck now by the thought that perhaps his students knew more about the world, certainly more about Moazzamabad, than he did.

He had only known Rasoolpur, and even here, he had only been interested in Shabbir Manzil. A dull anger with himself made his head and heart heavy, and his eyes smart. A wasted life.

And then they were at Rudrapur and Rafiq's thoughts came back to the present. They had thrown him out of Shabbir Manzil, and he had decided that he would leave on his feet and not on his knees, but now, outside Ajmal Khan's house, he found his courage faltering. He didn't really know what he was doing. It was the presence of Rustam that decided things for him. Now that he had come all the way here, he couldn't turn around without doing something.

'Stay here,' he told Rustam, his words more assertive than his tone. 'I won't be long.'

He pressed the doorbell but nothing happened. He tried again, and still there was no response. He knocked then, but it was a soft sound and summoned nobody. Frustrated, he pulled out a coin, and using the edge, knocked repeatedly on the metal door handle, finally making enough noise that he heard somebody say, 'Who is it?'

'Rafiq,' he said loudly. 'Rafiq Ansari.'

'Wait a minute.' And then Ajmal Khan opened the door.

'As salaam aleikum, Rafiq,' he said. 'What are you doing here?'

'I'm resigning from my job, Khan sahib,' Rafiq blurted out. Then, because he had been rude, he mumbled, 'Wa aleikum as salaam,' wishing peace in reply to Ajmal Khan's silence and look of mild confusion.

Ajmal Khan could hardly say he was surprised. Ahmad Saeed had phoned him an hour ago to say that he hadn't realized Rafiq had only a second-class degree in his BEd, not a first, and maybe that wasn't quite the required qualification for a teaching job at the college. Ajmal Khan had resisted, saying that there were few teachers with a BEd degree of whatever class in Moazzamabad, and even those few were either teaching at the old Halloway College or at H.D. Aggarwal College, where the pay was far better. But of course that wasn't what Ahmad Saeed had called up to say, and certainly he wasn't interested in what Ajmal Khan would have to say in Rafiq's defence. Realizing this halfway into the conversation, Ajmal Khan had simply made soft, affirmative noises while Ahmad Saeed continued talking about the suitability, or really the lack thereof, of Rafiq continuing to teach in his current job. At the end, because he knew that Ahmad Saeed would never be so gauche as to suggest it himself, Ajmal Khan had said, 'Maybe it would be best to review his case. In fact, although we had hired him, there is a clause in the contract that allows us to reconsider such cases, and if what you say is correct, which, since you are the person saying it, is not to be doubted, then Rafiq would have to be dismissed from his job by the end of this session, in a couple of months.'

'A couple of months?' Ahmad Saeed asked. 'It will take that long?'

'Procedures have to be followed,' Ajmal Khan said. He was happy to bend with the wind but if he didn't assert himself the managing committee would ride roughshod over him whenever they chose. 'We wouldn't want a court case against the college, would we?'

'He would never dare,' Ahmad Saeed exclaimed, but there was an edge of doubt in his voice.

'We wouldn't want to take that chance. The reputation of a college is its greatest asset. After all, that is why we are firing him, isn't it?'

The silence that followed was too long, and Ajmal Khan feared he had gone too far. He had to be careful here. Despite having lived in Moazzamabad for seven years now he was still an outsider, his position never fully secure. He couldn't afford sarcasm. Hurriedly he added, 'And I think I have the perfect candidate to replace Rafiq.'

'Do what you think is correct,' Ahmad Saeed said, a little restrained now. 'I will support you.'

'Thank you, Ahmad Saeed sahib,' Ajmal Khan gushed.

And now here was Rafiq, and he wanted to resign. Who was Ajmal Khan to refuse him?

Still he said, 'It's not so simple. There is paperwork.'

And when Rafiq said nothing, Ajmal Khan added, 'And you have to give at least three months' notice.'

Again Rafiq was quiet. He hadn't thought this far ahead; he had just wanted to do something about this feeling within him, to tear the shadow of Shabbir Manzil off his life.

'Let me speak to the managing committee,' Ajmal Khan said at last, put out by Rafiq's silence. 'Maybe I can convince them to let you go by the end of the month.'

'I'm willing to work to the end of the term,' Rafiq said finally, thinking belatedly of his students.

'Yes,' Ajmal Khan nodded sagely, 'yes, I think that might be for the best.'

'Thank you, Khan sahib,' Rafiq said, and because there was not a trace of gratitude in his voice, just relief at a bitter task done, and because Ajmal Khan resented the fact that Rafiq had been a good teacher, a far better teacher than his nephew would make, the principal replied bitterly, 'You *should* be thankful, Rafiq, it's a good habit to learn.'

Rafiq stiffened at the remark, and without saying a farewell, turned and left.

In reality, though, should he have expected anything more from Ajmal Khan? The man had treated him with condescension and sarcasm throughout the time they had known each other—a small man deeply conscious of being in a position of power. Why should that change because Shaista was dead and Rafiq was trying to recover a sense of honour that he had never had?

No, Ajmal Khan's reaction was no surprise. The real surprise was still waiting for him.

He didn't know what he had expected from his parents. Maybe some criticism of how he had cut off nearly all contact with them—criticism blunted by sympathy for his sudden loss. But he had no expectations. He wasn't fully conscious of anything, and was working on instinct rather than thought.

'You're a fool,' his father said. He said it softly, late at night, at the tail end of dinner when Rafiq's mother had stopped serving the men and was sitting down to eat her own meal.

'You're a fool. Why fight with Ahmad Saeed sahib? Why throw away your job?' his father asked. 'You had a good place for yourself. Your mother could brag to her relatives that you lived in Shabbir Manzil and taught at a college, and you have thrown it all away.'

Rafiq's mother raised her head at the end of that, and Rafiq, glancing her way, knew that she cared little about these things. It was his father who had gloried in his son's newfound standing, and now, under the guise of practicality, was complaining that they had slipped down the social ladder once again. *So I'm my father's son after all*, he thought to himself, and there was a touch of amusement in that.

'It's time for the isha prayers,' Rafiq said, and excused himself.

'Bowing to God is all well and good,' his father grumbled, 'but prayers don't fill your stomach.'

But he was wrong about that.

After the late-night prayers Rafiq didn't feel like returning to his parents' house, at least not immediately. He could have read from one of the copies of the Quran set in the niches, instead he just sat in a corner, counting the beads of a rosary but saying no prayer except Shaista's name.

'As salaam aleikum, beta,' the imam's greeting broke into his thoughts. 'How are you?'

'Wa aleikum as salaam, Maulana sahib,' Rafiq replied. He should have answered, *Alhamdulliallah*—praise be to God, all is well—but he couldn't. 'I have lost my wife, Maulana sahib, and I have lost my job. I asked you to pray for me once, for a job, and God gave me more than that. Maybe I was ungrateful and I have lost them both.'

Rafiq found that he was weeping, and wiped his face with his free hand. He felt ashamed, but it had happened too suddenly for him to control himself. At least there was only Qayoom sahib here in the mosque. Everybody else had left.

The imam lowered himself to sit cross-legged in front of Rafiq. He didn't reach out to touch Rafiq but said in his measured tones, 'God will provide.'

'Will He?' Rafiq demanded. 'Will He really provide?'

The imam shook his head at the anger, refusing to let the gentle smile slip from his face. 'Tell me, what were the first words of the Quran revealed to the Prophet, peace be upon Him?'

Rafiq shook his head. He knew, but right now he couldn't remember.

'Recite. Recite, in the name of God who gave Man the pen and taught him what he knew not,' the imam quoted, and Rafiq nodded.

'Allah has commanded that mankind be taught,' the imam continued. 'Aren't Muslims illiterate in today's world?

Don't they want to be taught? Aren't you a teacher? Isn't what you do, why you do it, an act of providence? Isn't the fact that there are thousands of poor who wish to be taught providence? Hasn't God provided?'

At last the imam reached out and touched Rafiq's hand, the one clutching the rosary. 'There are other places to teach, not as prestigious as Alvi College perhaps, and they won't pay you as much, but God has provided.'

'And what about Shaista?' Rafiq asked bitterly, the tears streaking his face. But to that the imam had no answer, or if he did, he kept it to himself.

BOOK TWO

8

Jamaal grew up between a maulana and a mullah. While his father searched for a job, he stayed for much of the day and studied with the imam, Maulana Qayoom. The first few years after Shaista's death were the most difficult for Rafiq. The jobs available were few and far between, and even Maulana Qayoom's reference didn't get him very far. The Islamic schools that had vacancies looked on him with some suspicion. He had no religious training or background, and was often caught flat-footed when asked about a point of religious doctrine.

After three failed interviews, the imam counselled him to spend two months on tabligh, travelling with a band of Muslims across the country to preach. Except it wasn't really preaching, it was *dawah*, invitation, proselytization. The odd thing was that the dawah was largely to Muslims who never had the time to attend the prayers even if the mosque was a few minutes' walk from their front door. He travelled with a group that went first to a mosque in Ghaziabad and from there to a series of other mosques in the little towns around Lucknow, even passing through

Tufailganj where Ismat Sharif lived.

Rafiq found some comfort when he heard that Shaista's brother rarely attended prayers, and that the local imam blamed the misfortunes of the Sharif household on the fact that they had forgotten they were Muslim. Wasn't it the same with Shabbir Manzil? Hadn't they too, in their arrogance, denied their faith and identity and addressed their petitions to the government, to the powers that were made by men and were, therefore, fallible?

In the group with which he travelled Rafiq found a number of people like him, who had only recently realized that they were bound by something deeper. One of them had lost a brother in a riot in Meerut; others claimed that their Muslim names made potential employers wince and look away. It was a bad time for the economy and stupid to be a visible minority of any sort.

After a few unsuccessful attempts to land a middle-level job at a local factory, one of the men, Haris, had recently forged papers which misspelled his name as 'Harish'. Since his last name was Chaudhary, carrying no religious significance, a little smudge on his birth certificate would make him safely employable. Haris told Rafiq this in confidence, adding that he was sure his application would go through this time. He had paid the requisite bribes to the right people; only his name had been standing in the way. 'One of the clerks handling my paperwork helped me out. He told me that it didn't matter if I padded the folder with hundred-rupee bills, his supervisor wouldn't hire a Muslim. He also told me where documents and certificates could be "manufactured"!' Haris laughed.

'Isn't that wrong?' Rafiq asked, feeling a little uneasy, as if by listening to this, and being expected to keep it confidential, he was somehow complicit in the forgery.

'Wrong?' Haris's eyes narrowed. 'I'll tell you what is wrong. Having to run from door to door begging, *that's* wrong. Destroying your pride is wrong. Having to hang your head before your wife and children is wrong. This is nothing.'

Then, shaking his head Haris said, 'You know what your problem is, Rafiq? You care too much about what people will say.'

Rafiq looked away, but Haris's guess was painfully close to the truth.

'Are you married?' Haris asked.

'My wife died a few months ago.'

'Oh, I'm sorry to hear that ... And children?'

'I have a son, Jamaal.'

'Where is he?'

'He's staying at the madrassah in Moazzamabad.'

'Don't you want to take care of him?' Haris asked.

And at that Rafiq looked up, suddenly angry.

Haris laughed lightly. 'You do, don't you? Well then all this doesn't matter too much, does it?'

'I don't want to lie,' Rafiq said lamely.

Haris made an exasperated noise. 'Listen, you can't expect the world to comply with your wishes.'

When Rafiq didn't reply Haris added, 'There's a simple trick that will help you get a job at an Islamic school.'

Rafiq didn't like the word 'trick', but he listened.

'Just be angry,' Haris said. 'Rant and rave. Talk about the grand tragedies, about oppression, *zulm*, riots and murder. Grow your beard a little longer and miss no opportunity to raise your voice against the suffering of Muslims. It's what the mullahs do all the time.'

Rafiq nodded reluctantly.

Haris threw up his hands. 'You're an intelligent man, and you'll do a good job teaching, what does it matter if you have to scare the people interviewing you a little to get the job. If they ask about some vague point of law, tell them—"The police shoot Muslims every other day, and *this* is what you are worried about?"'

'It's not as if it is untrue,' Rafiq mumbled.

Haris laughed softly. 'As long as they haven't shot *us*.'

At the next interview, in a little school newly established at Hamirpur, fifteen kilometres from Moazzamabad, Rafiq kept his face stern. His beard had grown, filling the hollows of his face. He knew snatches of Islamic doctrine now, and when they quizzed him about it, he answered the questions readily enough at first, and then, taking a deep breath, he said, 'You know my credentials. I have taught at a much better place than this. I even sacrificed part of my salary when they were conducting vasectomies during the Emergency on poor Muslims. I have proved myself as both a teacher and a Muslim, what exactly is it that you are trying to determine?'

It caught them up short, the blunt words maybe, or the fierceness of the tone. There was a mumbled conversation among the three men who were sitting across the table.

After a while the eldest of them said, 'My apologies, Ansari sahib, but we are leaving you in charge of our children, after all. We shall let you know by the end of the week.'

'Thank you,' Rafiq said. He kept his face stiff, unwilling to betray the tension he felt inside. There was still some money left in his savings, but not for much longer, and he cursed Haris for the bad advice. There was no need to pretend to be so hard, but now that he'd spoken as he had, there was nothing to be done about it. 'As salaam aleikum,' he said as he left.

Two days later he was informed that he had got the job. Rafiq knew better than to celebrate. He went to the mosque, and after thanking the imam for his help, immediately, and very publicly, offered prayers in thanks.

He was in the hands of God now.

It was a disguise that grew on him. Very much like the time when he had confronted Ahmad Saeed, Rafiq realized that the anger he expressed, even if he believed none of it, gave him a sort of power. Now that he had lost access to Shabbir Manzil, he found that he liked to sit among the serious people at the mosque after the prayers and discuss the trials and tribulations of Muslims. And just as a memory for Urdu poetry had carved out a place for him at Shabbir Manzil, his ear for a finely turned phrase made him a voice to listen to when people talked of riots and revolution. It was funny, though, how much he had to thank Haris for, because it wasn't just in job interviews that well-articulated anger gave you some space. He spoke rarely, but just once in a while he would trail out some pithy argument, said in controlled rage, about the state of Muslims, in India, in all the world. It gained him the kind of respect that none of his social climbing had.

As for young Jamaal, even after his father found employment, he spent much of his free time at the mosque, either being taught his Arabic and Urdu by the imam or playing with the other children, and it was there that he first heard the name his father had earned. Rafiq was completing the non-obligatory prayers one day and Jamaal was waiting for him, watching a group of prosperous-looking gentlemen, as they stood chatting. One of them turned his head and noticed the child staring at them.

'Hello, young man,' he said, his long mane bobbing. Although Jamaal found the person vaguely familiar, he was too shy to speak. He was only eight years old, and the three years after his mother's death had taught him only the value of silence.

'Hello,' the person repeated. His mane reminded Jamaal of the picture of a lion he had stuck on his pencil box, and imagining this strange man as a scrawny, undersized lion, standing on two legs and with no tail to speak of, Jamaal had to hide a smile.

'Ah, so the little one laughs,' the strange man said, and Jamaal was about to ask him about the vastness of his hair, and where his tail had gone, when one of the other men turned to see what was happening. And maybe he was the real lion, because the long-maned man's smile narrowed until it was hardly even there. But Jamaal wasn't afraid. There was something very familiar about the larger man;

Jamaal could not see this new man's hands, but he felt he knew what they looked like and how they felt.

'So, Khan sahib, you've spotted one of the next generation of poets?' the larger man said, and he might have had a hint of a smile on his face because now the long-haired man let his smile reappear. Then the larger man looked beyond Jamaal and his features, relaxed and generous till now, tightened swiftly with revulsion. 'Here comes that mullah, Rafiq.'

And with those words the little knot of men wound down their conversation and moved towards the exit of the mosque. Jamaal turned to see who they were referring to and saw his father coming their way. He wanted to call the men back to say that they had it wrong. Yes, the man approaching them was called Rafiq, but he was not a mullah, he was a teacher at the small school in Hamirpur. But they fled so quickly that he had no time to say anything, and when his father came and rested a hand on his shoulder, there was no need to say anything. Father and son, neither was much for words.

Afterwards, when he was at home, Jamaal took out his blue plastic pencil box and looked again at the lion stuck on it, and realized that none of the men had actually looked like lions. In the picture, little as it was, the great cat stood upright and unafraid, its head raised in challenge. It seemed like the master of all it surveyed, not one who would scuttle away from any man, mullah or not.

Only later did Jamaal find out that the large man was his uncle, Ahmad Saeed Shabbir, the cousin of his dead mother.

But that was all he found out. The only time he saw the older man was at Friday prayers, standing far in front among the rows of prestige just behind the imam. Jamaal stood with the children, far to the back so their whispering, pinching and other games wouldn't disturb the elders in their prayer. His father stood somewhere in between, ahead of the unmarried men, but far behind the prestigious first few rows, and it seemed that Rafiq was glad, and would have stood even further back, among the children, so that he could be close to his son. But such display of affection was considered unseemly in men, and Rafiq would only come to Jamaal after the prayers, rest his hand on the boy's shoulder, and they would make the trip to the cemetery to pray at Jamaal's mother's grave.

9

There is more to being a mullah than prayer. It took a while for Jamaal to understand the difference, although he had always known instinctively that there was one. People called the imam 'Maulana sahib' in deference to the obvious markers of his faith, but they would never have referred to him as a mullah. It would have been an insult of sorts. Maulana Jalali Qayoom was the imam of one of the oldest mosques in the city; he had social standing, prestige. He was no mere mullah.

When Jamaal understood that, he understood much, or as much as the mind of a boy who spent most of his time listening and little talking, and who was approaching his teenage years, could understand. This was about power, about honour, and ultimately about wealth.

Later, he would learn more. That it wasn't money that distinguished the imam and made him more than a mullah. No, he had little enough, but still he had enough, and if he needed more it would have been provided. It isn't necessary to add that it would have been the wealthy families that would have provided, because who else had the means?

They would have provided because the imam was necessary, the mosque was necessary, an order was necessary on top of which the rich and powerful could find their place.

In the end what is the point of power if people don't admire you for it? What is the use of wealth if others don't envy you for it? You can't eat gold, but you can live off your pride. For that you need a community composed of both the rich and those who desire to be rich. You need a guardian of morality who whispers the requests of the needy into the ears of the wealthy so that they can be generous, all in the name of God's grace.

Mullahs, though, were a different breed. They had no mosque, just a message. Their piety had a smell, like the sweat of those who can afford soap but not perfume. It was an offence to the well-cultivated sensibilities of the rich, making their nostrils curl in disgust. Worst of all, the mullahs didn't listen, and they certainly didn't whisper. A mullah had the Word of God, and didn't care to murmur it gently, nor did he care to have its nuances explained to him, especially the parts that excused the important folk from the petty obligations of prayer and other such minor details.

Still, what did it matter? Without a mosque, without the favour of the wealthy, a mullah was a mere man, even if his voice was more insistent than that of most.

That Jamaal understood all this instinctively was not only because he had spent all his life listening. The more important reason was that he was powerless, a cipher in the system that cared little for mullahs, or their sons.

Nothing teaches a person the rules of power better than being excluded from it, and Jamaal knew all about that. And he learned about it at the same place as his father had: St Jude's.

Jamaal gained admission in the sixth standard at St Jude's, the excitement of it making his eleven-year-old body tremble with joy. But it was short-lived, for it was here that he learned soon enough what it meant to be poor. The school had originally been set up by German missionaries in 1904 as Wolfsson School, but was taken over by the government during the First World War. It had finally ended up in the hands of the Gill family, of fine old Sikh ancestry, who were gifted a large plot of land in the region for their loyalty to the British Empire. No better fate could have befallen the school. The Gills were rich enough to ignore the profits from it, little as they were, and old Harinder Gill, the patriarch of the family, had himself been one of the first students of St Jude's. A committed Anglophile, he made sure that St Jude's had all that it needed for a thorough, if Spartan, education emphasizing the values of an English public school.

Whether out of his anglicized sense of fair play—and his anglicized ways had found their first expression in the change of the school's name—or just because he didn't need to favour the children of the rich, Harinder Gill instituted entrance exams for the school, and based the fee structure on the income of the parents of the students who made it through the exams. This meant that middle-class parents who dreamed of sending their children to St Jude's could now actually afford to. This legacy was what Rafiq had benefitted from, and now Jamaal.

But privilege, or the lack of it, will show. Although the entrance exam was open to all and even a mullah could send his son to St Jude's, the hurdles of wealth were not just in the income of the rich, but in the attitude of their children as well. Within the confines of the school the politics of wealth was indulged in as viciously by the children as their parents played it outside. But maybe that is how things were meant to be. The children were training for their adult lives and if they didn't learn how to recognize who mattered and who didn't, what good would their education be?

But it was a stiff-upper-lip school, and the teachers ever vigilant, and the rules of the game needed to be as subtle. The first rule was to do with wealth, of course, and how to flaunt it. Since everybody was forced to wear the school uniform, it was the accessories that counted: the shoes and the stationery. To own a cheap plastic pencil box, as Jamaal did, marked one out as somebody to be avoided. The stickers that Jamaal had covered the plastic with made it worse for him. You could easily see that the stickers were of the cheapest quality, and even those were old, their condition as threadbare as Jamaal's chances of social acceptability.

The game of exclusion and mockery was usually played out most successfully in the gym class. The well-fed children of the rich glowed healthily next to their scrawny, pigeon-chested rivals. Even if physique was a gift of genetics rather than of wealth, the quality of running shoes clearly divided those who walked on air from those whose heels barely rose above the dirt of their existence.

Jamaal wore canvas sneakers of the cheap variety that lasted barely one season, with rubber soles so thin that pebbles would punch their way through them if Jamaal ran too hard. But why would he run swiftly anyway? There was no prize awaiting him at the finish line. Being a winner requires more than just being first in a race: a victory is never quite that unless there are people who will acknowledge your triumph. It was the reason Jamaal never stood first in any of his exams. He had never excelled at anything enough to attract attention.

Except once. It had happened right at the beginning, before he learned how to behave.

Jamaal had been taught by Rafiq to do well, and Rafiq was a good teacher at least, a man who valued his students' achievements. Jamaal's early education had been studded with gifts and encouragement. Nothing too expensive, just a sticker here, a candy there, and often enough only a dazzling smile from a silent but proud father. At school it was different. In his first social sciences test Jamaal had answered every question correctly, even getting an extra point for a bonus question, earning a score of 21 out of 20 points. His father had been delighted and just before the maghrib prayers he had taken Jamaal to the local stationery shop and bought him his first fountain pen. The boy had spent all evening playing with the pen, filling it with ink, squirting it out, practising his signature endlessly, even attempting the temerity to write his father's name.

The pen didn't go unnoticed at school. Every little change was noticed, and anyway it wasn't as if Jamaal hid it. He wrote with a flourish, each move of his hand making the gold of the pen glitter. The next day was gym class, and three of the boys stayed afterwards to talk to Jamaal. They were openly admiring of his skills in social sciences, and Jamaal was happy to brag. He didn't notice that Arun was not there. He should have. Arun was the one who usually came first in class, and these three, Amit, Saurav and Rahul, were his closest friends.

There was a moment when Jamaal felt something odd. Rahul had been praising him to the skies, and said, 'You could be part of our study group. You could lead us.'

A sudden silence descended on the group. Although Rahul had proposed the idea, it had lost steam even before he finished saying it, the last words coming out less as a statement than as a question already gone wrong.

Amit added, reluctantly, 'We meet on Saturday mornings at Ruby's.'

Jamaal knew the name of the restaurant. It was the most fashionable restaurant in Moazzamabad. Actually, it was the only one; all the rest were glorified dhabas or other greasy eateries. Jamaal had never been there, of course. But he had stared curiously at the rich people of the city walking within its portals. He had no idea what it cost to eat there. He had never thought about it. What was the use, when he knew that he could never afford it? And how did one behave inside a place like Ruby's? How did one sit, what did one ask for and how? There were, Jamaal knew, a hundred different ways to fail in a place like that.

'Saturday morning?' he asked falteringly.

The others nodded slowly, unsure, and that gave Jamaal time to think up an excuse. 'My Urdu lessons—I go to the mosque for my Urdu lessons on Saturday,' he blurted.

And at that they all smiled, suddenly liberated. For no reason Jamaal started laughing, and the others joined in. He was so relieved that his classmates had turned out so much more welcoming than the children in Rasoolpur.

Even when he got back to his class Jamaal didn't notice anything odd, except that Amit, Saurav and Rahul immediately left his side and made their way to where Arun was sitting, smiling contentedly to himself. And then school was over, gym class being the last session for the day.

It was only when he reached home and took out his books to do his homework that Jamaal found out what had happened. When he opened the fountain pen, ink splashed out of the cap all over his shirt and trousers. He leapt to his feet, trying to save his notebook. His clothes could be washed, but not the paper. Luckily he had sat on the floor instead of his bed, and he ran to get a cloth to mop up the ink. He filled a bucket of water, and soaking the cloth, he carefully cleaned the mess, and then, sprinkling some washing powder on the floor, he scrubbed the tiles until the stains were almost gone, leaving only a slight darkness in the cracks.

When he turned his attention to the pen, he found that there was no nib. It had been snapped off, as if somebody had taken the pen and smashed it, nib first, into the ground with as much force as he could muster. It was destroyed beyond any hope of recovery, and when he realized that Jamaal started to cry.

He couldn't tell his father—what could his father do? He himself owned only one fountain pen, an old one. He couldn't afford to buy Jamaal another one, especially if even that one would be broken by the boys in school. And if Jamaal complained, what would he say? What proof did he have? Just that Amit and Saurav and Rahul had praised him, that they had talked to him like a friend, an equal? And even if the teachers believed him, would that make him safer, could he ever afford to bring the fruit of his achievements, the proof of his father's pride, to school, knowing that someone would find a way to destroy it? A gift was no use if you lived forever in fear of what might happen to it.

So Jamaal learned that there was a price to success, and the price wasn't simply hard work. He also realized that he wasn't a fighter, that he didn't have the courage to confront his tormentors. He could only bend before them, not challenge them in any way. He understood then why his father never protested about being called a mullah behind his back. He understood who his father was, and also that he was his father's son, a mullah's son, and a coward. He lay down on the cool ground, curled his body around the broken pen and wept.

10

Jamaal found not just truth at St Jude's, but also a friend: Khalid the bastard.

It's hard to say exactly what their relationship was, or indeed what friendship meant to either of them. Part of it was just that neither of them had any other friends, and perhaps that explains the nature of their relationship: the soft, almost secret greeting exchanged in the morning, a lunch shared when Khalid hadn't brought anything, or a cup of tea that Khalid paid for though he didn't look like he came from a home of any considerable means. This was how it was; there were hardly any words exchanged, and there were no shared interests. What there was, though nobody knew this and neither of them quite acknowledged it either, was the complicity of a criminal and his accomplice.

So, perhaps it wasn't friendship. But then, how do you define friendship? Is it good fortune or only a privilege, a gift for those blessed with good sense and an even temper? Either way, what can it really mean to two young boys in Moazzamabad, each carrying the mark of his father's sins and mother's death?

Khalid was, of course, the son of Shakeel Shabbir, the second son of that grand house, the son in whose company no respectable woman would be seen. And if disrespectable women found themselves in his vicinity, well, everybody knew how he would act. Wasn't Khalid living proof of that? The boy had his father's features, had had them since birth, and became more like him as the years went by, acquiring the same fleshy lips, the floppy hair, even the odd mannerism of pulling at his earlobe when he was lost in thought. Everybody could see that he was Shakeel's son—they just didn't know who his mother was.

Shabbir Manzil always maintained that it had been a secret marriage, that Shakeel's mother had come from an orthodox, even an ultra-orthodox, Shia family in Lucknow who disapproved violently of all Sunni Muslims such as the Shabbirs. And the poor woman had died in childbirth, which was the great, disorienting tragedy of Shakeel's life.

But the story hardly silenced the doubters and the merely curious. Why would a Shia woman fall in love with Shakeel? And if her family was ultra-orthodox, how did she meet him in the first place? And why did this only become known after her death? And now that she was dead, couldn't at least her family be named, so that others, genuinely sympathetic maybe, could offer their condolences?

No. The story raised far more questions than it answered. The only reason nobody dared ask Shakeel was that he was as quick with his fists as he was rumoured to be oily in his ways. And Shabbir Manzil said nothing else. So the mystery persisted, as did the rumours and insinuations, and the occasional insult. There was no real need to please the man; everybody knew that the wealth and power was vested in the person of Ahmad Saeed, who shared none of it with his wayward younger brother. The people of the mohalla called Khalid exactly what they thought the son of a philanderer should be called: a bastard. It was a constant whisper in Khalid's world, barely heard but always there: *haraamzaada*, bastard. But nobody was willing to explain to him what it meant, no matter how much he asked.

Ignorance is always a matter of choice. You can choose to see, and you can choose to listen. But isn't it a miracle of God that it is always easier to hear and bear what people are saying than it is to see the truth? We may shut our eyes, but we can never close our ears; and even if people can choose to close their mouths and silence their tongues, they seldom do.

Khalid became familiar with the title of bastard long before he was told anything about it by his father. And whatever he was told, he kept strictly to himself. He had been laughed at enough in his life to want to invite more mockery by opening his mouth and protesting his mother's innocence. Or maybe Khalid understood the peculiarity of the title. A bastard is not so much a sinner himself as a product of sin. Or the product, many would say, of wayward love, or rebel love, or even the legitimate, virile passion of a man who will obey no rules. And in that case the title can also be a form of praise, an abusive sort of praise, but praise nonetheless.

Khalid, never quite respectable, yet never entirely rejected, was always on the edge of things, breaking rules in a lackadaisical manner that displayed not so much a wish to cause mischief as an inability to follow any convention at all. For someone born outside the law, outside of society, what did it mean that the teacher wanted homework done? What sense did it make, the demand that students should be presentably turned out, with their shirts ironed, nails clipped and hair neatly cut? Khalid could never follow any of these instructions. He would try; at the beginning of each year, he would try, but within a couple of months his notebooks would become scarred and leprous with abuse, a seam would open up in his shirt, and his shoelaces would habitually come undone.

The teachers tried to do their bit, some out of concern for the boy, others because it hurt their ego the way he flouted all the norms. It had little impact. Khalid would suffer the punishments with mulish indifference. He would present his hand to be hit with the teacher's slim disciplining rod. He would stand in the corner, silently, when ordered to do so. He would spend the recess time shut up in the classroom completing the homework that he had forgotten to do. Khalid simply didn't care. He had no friends whose shame could affect him, and he cared nothing for the teachers' encouragement. There was no pain that they could subject him to that would make him wince and resolve to change.

Though, in fact, he was a bright child, even a talented one. His geography and biology teachers raved about the fine detail with which he drew his diagrams and maps. His maths teachers had also come to realize that although Khalid may be dozing off, or playing with an insect in the back row, his understanding of numbers was far better than students two years his senior. But these came instinctively to Khalid, he did not have to work at them. He understood them at a gut level and simply produced what he considered natural. It was the rest of the stuff, the social science classes and the English lessons, that he couldn't quite grasp.

After a while the school just gave up. It wasn't as if he was disruptive; there wasn't any real damage that he could do—for all his spunk and devil-may-care attitude, he was a loner, not part of any gang. The other students, in any case, had realized that there were things that he could get away with that they shouldn't even attempt. Even if they survived the harsh scolding, or punishment, that would come their way, they had parents at home who would pick up where the teachers had left off. Khalid had no such fear. His father would come to the school if the teachers called. He would even cuff Khalid, and yell at him, but it was all an act, a performance by father and son for a society that cared nothing for either.

Jamaal should have been the exact opposite. He was a quiet child, one of those who never raised his hand in any class, with the possible exception of English literature, and never made a performance or a fuss. His homework was always done on time, and if the teacher asked him a question, he would always have the answer. On the surface, at least, Jamaal was an ideal student—a child who came to be taught, who listened and learned. Except that no teacher really liked him. In fact, they hardly noticed him. For most of them he was only a name in the attendance register or on top of an exam paper; he made no further impact on them. Maybe they understood that just as Khalid cared nothing for social norms and knew at some deep level that he would remain just a poor bastard, Jamaal was always going to be a mullah's son, no matter what he did.

The two boys met just before the English class. Jamaal's English class.

After the incident of the pen, Jamaal had retreated into himself, but he had watched and learned that no one particularly cared about the English class, no one except the girls, and they were not the sort to bully Jamaal physically. Of course, they had their own system of humiliation and exclusion. A snide remark and a snigger could stay with some unfortunate for weeks. It would be whispered behind a back, but if the victim turned to look there would only be a few girls, all prim and proper in their uniforms, not one of them showing any emotion at all. But Jamaal was too low on the social scale for this to have much effect on him. He could afford to ignore their dislike most of the time, and be invisible. This was necessary.

It was true that Rafiq had expected much from his son, and just once in a while Jamaal needed to make his father proud, and the English class was good enough for that. The subject may not have mattered to the other boys, who were too busy trying to prove themselves in the sciences, but to him it was a safe way of ensuring he had something with which to occasionally make his father happy. It wasn't quite so simple, of course. He had to be careful, too. The girls were related to some of the boys by blood, community or social standing. This was Moazzamabad, after all, and there were only a handful of families that mattered, and most of them had some children studying at St Jude's. The boys didn't care if Jamaal did all right in a girlie subject, but he had to make sure it was never interpreted as humiliating their sisters. That would be going too far.

This was how Jamaal felt and measured the walls of his prison, day by day, and figured out to the last half-span of a hand what kind of freedom he was allowed. And during that voyage of discovery, he also discovered Khalid.

He shouldn't have, not really. Even if Khalid was from the same mohalla, he was still a year senior to Jamaal, and at such an age a year is a boundary more real than the borders of many states. But they met through a criminal conspiracy—and if you are already breaking laws, what do social conventions matter?

Jamaal was sitting in the classroom during lunch break, working on his English lesson. There was no point in going outside to play, when all he could do was play alone. Khalid sauntered into the room. He saw Jamaal, but it didn't give him pause; instead he quickly went through pencil box after pencil box on the desks in the front row. Jamaal could only watch from his seat near the back of the class and admire the smooth, silent efficiency of Khalid's fingerwork.

Suddenly Khalid stopped. He had just opened Saurav's pencil box. He reached in and pulled out a single currency note. Jamaal was too far away to see it clearly, and Khalid's fingers too quick to give him much of a chance, but it looked like a large note, maybe fifty or even a hundred rupees. Khalid looked up and met Jamaal's eyes. He didn't smile, or show emotion of any kind, but there was an understanding of sorts reached between them. Then Jamaal went back to his work, and Khalid disappeared.

11

The noise of the children returning from the lunch break sounded unnaturally loud to Jamaal, but nothing happened. Saurav didn't need his pencil box for the first class, nor the next.

It was only at the beginning of the third class, the last one before the end of school, that Saurav opened his pencil box. Jamaal saw him pause, and start rummaging through the box. He had been watching Saurav so intently that it was a relief that the theft had been discovered, and he lowered his eyes so that Saurav wouldn't turn around and catch him looking. But he heard the low hiss of conversation as Saurav turned and whispered urgently to Rahul.

'Rahul, Saurav,' the teacher asked sternly, 'are you sharing secrets or is there something you'd like to discuss with the rest of the class?'

Now Jamaal could look up. Everybody was staring at Saurav and Rahul. It was Rahul who answered, his voice stiff. 'Ma'am, some money is missing from Saurav's pencil box.'

'Are you sure?' Mrs Tripathi asked Saurav severely.

This was too much for Saurav, and he turned, teary-eyed, and pointed his finger at Jamaal. '*He* stole it! That thief stole my money,' and having made the accusation, he started weeping uncontrollably.

Jamaal had been expecting it, but he hadn't known how he would react. He felt the shock, the blood draining from his face, but he sat stock-still. He didn't have any words to respond.

'Saurav!' Mrs Tripathi exclaimed in anger and then, as the class burst into excited chatter, she banged her ruler on her desk. 'All of you, if you don't start behaving yourselves in *one* minute, I will cancel your lunch break for the rest of the week.'

It took some time but the classroom subsided into silence, with only Saurav hiccupping in anger. They knew from experience that Mrs Tripathi was not to be trifled with. 'Saurav, do you have any idea what you are saying?'

'He was right here, ma'am,' Saurav burbled. 'We all went out to play after having lunch, and he just stayed here, and he stole my money.'

Mrs Tripathi looked up and met Jamaal's eyes, but he still couldn't find anything to say. It was Mrs Tripathi who said, 'Jamaal always stays here during the lunch break.' There was an odd note in her voice, something that Jamaal couldn't identify. If he could have believed it possible coming from someone as stern as Mrs Tripathi, he would have said it was sympathy, or at least pity, that hid in her tone, making it flat but still full of questions.

'My money was in the pencil box before I left,' Saurav

insisted, 'and it was gone when I came back. It was him, I know it. It was that dirty little thief. He did it.'

'Saurav!' This time Mrs Tripathi's tone was much stricter, cutting through even Saurav's newfound sense of authority and shutting him up.

After a pause she said, 'I'm taking both of you to see the Principal. Arun, Ritika, take care of the classroom. If I hear even a whisper in the corridor, you will all regret it very much.'

Jamaal stood up, but his legs were trembling. He forced himself to be steady, gripping hard the ruler in his hand, and made his way forward. He could feel the eyes on the back of his neck and, despite Mrs Tripathi's threat, the insect buzz of whispering was clear in his ears.

'Do you want to leave your ruler behind?' Mrs Tripathi asked, but he shook his head, and she didn't insist.

It was only fifty yards across the playground to the Principal's office, but it was the longest walk that Jamaal had ever taken. Next to him he could hear the quick breathing of Saurav, somewhere between rage and tears. Jamaal didn't look at him. Even as they waited outside the office, Jamaal didn't turn to look at the other boy.

'You'll never get away with this,' Saurav hissed. 'I'll make you pay. My father will make your father pay.'

Jamaal flushed at that, but he didn't answer, and suddenly the door was open, Mrs Tripathi standing there, with the dark, round face of Mr Thomas visible over his desk just behind her.

'Tell the truth,' Mrs Tripathi said, and she glanced

sympathically at Jamaal, and he thought, *She knows. She knows about my guilt.*

His heart was beating so hard that he barely heard Mr Thomas say, 'Come in boys.'

He didn't invite them to sit, and they wouldn't have dared to anyway. Mr Thomas came from a family of Keralite priests who had spent their lives implementing the strict teachings of the Syrian Orthodox church. Although he had chosen to go into education instead, there was something about his face that told you he was a person who believed in sin and hellfire, and repentance that came from suffering a long, lingering death on the cross.

'Tell me,' Mr Thomas said, and Saurav did: that his father had given him a hundred-rupee note to buy a new tie and belt for his school uniform, and that it had been in his pencil box until before lunch, when everyone except Jamaal was out of the class. Saurav could have stopped there, but he might have thought that it wasn't enough, so he elaborated how Jamaal was a sneaking, cheating boy who didn't take part in any sports and spent his time making jealous comments on the pens and clothes and everything else that the other kids had. As he paused to draw breath, Mr Thomas raised a hand and asked, 'Did you check?'

The question caught Saurav open-mouthed. He didn't know what he was being asked.

'Did you check before you went out to play that your money was in the pencil box?'

'Yes,' Saurav said, but after a brief hesitation, and even

Jamaal understood that Saurav was lying. Mr Thomas said nothing, but he said nothing significantly, and that made Saurav defiant: 'Yes, I *did* check. Just before I finished lunch, before I went to the playground.' Turning towards Jamaal, he raised an accusing finger. 'He must have seen it then, he's always staring after us, the greedy little thief.'

'Mr Mukherjee,' Mr Thomas said firmly, 'I am sure you have been taught that pointing is rude.'

Saurav immediately lowered his finger but continued to glare at Jamaal.

'Your whole case, Mr Mukherjee,' Mr Thomas said, 'rests on the fact that Jamaal stayed in during the lunch break, that he was the only person who stayed there, and that you had left your money in your pencil box and it wasn't there when you returned. Is that correct?'

Saurav nodded. 'Yes, sir.'

'Do you often keep money in your pencil box?'

Saurav hesitated, and then said, 'Yes, sir, when I have any.'

'And Jamaal always stays in the classroom during the lunch break?'

'Yes, sir.'

'Can you explain to me then, Mr Mukherjee,' Mr Thomas asked, 'why, if Jamaal is the lying thief you say he is, he hasn't stolen your money before?'

Saurav was nonplussed for a while, and then blurted, 'But sir, there is always a first time.'

Mr Thomas nodded, and brought his hands together before him, the fingers interlocked. 'Yes, of course you're right, Mr Mukherjee. There is always a first time.' But as Saurav started to puff up in victory, he added, 'For example, this is the first time that I am hearing any accusations of wrongdoing by Jamaal. In the one and a half years that he has been with us, Jamaal has never given us cause for complaint. Unlike you, Mr Mukherjee, I might add.'

'But he stole my money!' exclaimed Saurav.

Now the Principal turned to Jamaal, and asked, 'What do you have to say to this, Mr Ansari?'

'I didn't steal his money, sir,' the words came out almost as a whisper, but Jamaal was surprised that they had come out at all. 'I didn't know he had hundred rupees, sir. I didn't take it. I've never held a hundred-rupee note in my life!'

He hadn't expected his voice to rise like that at the end, but it was true, all of it, especially the last, and telling the truth has an effect. Even Saurav started to look unsure.

Mr Thomas looked from one boy to the other, and said, 'Stealing is a very serious charge.'

'You can search my bag, sir,' Jamaal said, gaining confidence.

'He's just hidden it on himself,' Saurav said in desperation.

Jamaal faced the Principal and declared, 'If you want, sir, I'm willing to be searched.'

Mr Thomas turned to Saurav. 'Is that what you want, Mr Mukherjee?'

'Yes, sir,' Saurav said emphatically. 'Search him, his bag, his desk. I want him standing in his underpants so people can see what a thief he is.'

The Principal's eyes narrowed at the vicious triumph in Saurav's voice. 'Have they taught you *Othello* yet, Mr Mukherjee?'

Saurav shook his head, confused by the turn the conversation had taken. 'No, sir ... that's next year. This year we are studying *The Merchant of Venice*.'

'Hmm ...' Mr Thomas said. 'Maybe it might have made a difference if you'd been taught that. But still, what do you make of these lines?

Who steals my purse, steals trash; 'tis something, nothing;
'twas mine, 'tis his, and has been slave to thousands;
But he that filches from me my good name
Robs me of that which not enriches him
And makes me poor indeed.'

Saurav had nothing to say. Although Mr Thomas spoke the words slowly, and the boys had been taught Shakespeare, Saurav was in no state to make sense of the old-fashioned English.

'It means,' Mr Thomas explained, 'that while money is important, a reputation is far more precious, and the person who destroys another's reputation steals from him something that is more important than any amount of money can be.'

When Saurav said nothing, the Principal continued, 'Mr Mukherjee, you have accused Mr Ansari of being a thief. If it is true, and we shall find out soon enough as we go through Mr Ansari's belongings, then Mr Ansari will be punished for being a thief. But, if it is untrue, then you

have attacked something far more important, and have
committed a far greater crime by slandering your fellow
classmate who has done you no harm but whom you have
insulted and defamed before your classmates, your teacher
and your Principal. Do you understand me?'

Slowly Saurav nodded, but Mr Thomas sighed. 'No,
actually you don't. It is something that I will have to
explain to your parents, and to the rest of the school.'

Saurav paled at the mention of his parents, and Mr
Thomas moderated his tone to blunt the force of his next
words. 'If your accusation is untrue, Mr Mukherjee, you
will apologize to Mr Ansari before the whole school in the
next assembly, and you will explain why you are
apologizing.'

Then, for the first time, Jamaal felt sorry for Saurav, and
said, 'No, sir, that's not necessary.'

'I am the Principal, Mr Ansari,' Mr Thomas all but
shouted. 'I shall decide what is necessary.' Turning back to
Saurav, he asked, 'Mr Mukherjee, do you understand, and
do you still want to put Jamaal through a search?'

It was an unfair question. Saurav had committed himself
too much to back off now, but he didn't have the courage
to say it. He merely nodded.

'Very well, Mr Mukherjee,' the Principal said, 'very
well.'

12

Things changed for Jamaal after Saurav's public apology. It mattered little to the students what Mr Thomas said about reputation and accusations. The quote from *Othello* was familiar to the older children, but the meaning of the quote was dwarfed by the sight of Saurav Mukherjee apologizing to Jamaal Ansari. For most of them the lesson was about power, and they understood very well that Jamaal might not be powerful, but he wasn't powerless either. And maybe that was the essence of what the Principal was trying to teach them.

It didn't win Jamaal any friends. If anything, it made the rest of the children maintain their distance from him. He was all right with that; if no friends came close, then neither did his tormentors. It was a price he was willing to pay because his only loss was the fantasy of affection, nothing more, while he was spared the reality of humiliation.

He did make one friend, though, sort of, and that was of course Khalid. It happened quite unexpectedly, almost by chance. Jamaal no longer spent his time in the classroom during the lunch break, and instead went to the dining hall where, after finishing his meal, he would work on his assignments. There was always room for him to spread out his books where he sat, because nobody would sit at a table with him, just as nobody in his class would share a bench with him now.

Then, one day soon after Saurav's apology, Khalid sat down across him at the table, and signalled to the boy at the counter. 'Two teas, and a plate of gulab jamuns.'

When the tea and gulab jamuns were brought to the table, Khalid said, 'There's only one spoon here. There are two of us.' And that made Jamaal's throat close up with feeling. He hadn't known that the sweets were for him as well, along with the tea. He had never had them here before—he'd never had the money to afford them.

Khalid waited until the boy brought a second spoon, before digging in, and inviting Jamaal, gesturing with his spoon, to do so as well.

Did Jamaal become an accomplice when he picked up that second spoon, or was it when he tasted the sweet, or when he let Khalid pay? Until that moment only silence had stood between them—or bound them. They had said nothing to each other about that afternoon. But surely those gulab jamuns were bought with stolen money, with Saurav's money? Just as Jamaal had become part of the crime when he hadn't raised an alarm while Khalid was looking through pencil boxes to see what he could steal, now he was accepting his role, accepting a bribe, maybe, for keeping quiet afterwards.

But things are never that simple, of course. Especially

when it is a contract of silence, never acknowledged. When Khalid sat down and ordered that cup of tea he was also doing something else—sharing a table with a social outcast, and that too one who was a year junior to him. However unpopular Khalid himself might have been, the sheer fact of his seniority gave him a certain amount of power, and prestige, and he had set that aside so casually.

Nor was it a one-off. Every week, without fail, Khalid would sit down at the same table as Jamaal, and order a cup of tea, sometimes snacks. How could it be a bribe then, since Khalid ended up spending, in one- and two-rupee instalments, far more on Jamaal than the hundred rupees he had stolen from Saurav's pencil box? It wasn't as if Jamaal could help him get away with another such crime. In fact, after Saurav's money went missing many students had reported small thefts of the past. Everybody was on the lookout, and if Khalid carried on stealing it could only have been outside the school premises.

Jamaal was certain that the thieving was far from over. There were days when Khalid would be flushed with a kind of fever, and though he said nothing, didn't even smile, you could feel a glow of accomplishment in his eyes. And there would be a new pen in his pocket, or he'd be carrying a chocolate bar from which he ritually broke off some squares to pass across the table. Once, languidly, he stretched his arms, and Jamaal saw a watch that he knew he'd never seen on Khalid's wrist before that day.

It might be an art, thievery, a performance art that you can't share. Maybe that day, so long ago, Khalid had seen in Jamaal an audience, someone who would watch, and not say a word, who might even appreciate the sight of the law being casually broken, a bastard getting a bastard's revenge. And the tea, the sweets and the snacks were Khalid's way of thanking his audience. What is the point of artistry, after all, without appreciation? And Khalid wouldn't have been the first artist to pay for applause or admiration.

And Jamaal, what did *he* get from it all? Was he merely greedy, his friendship bought and sold for a cup of tea and the taste of syrupy sweetness on his lips? Was that the whole price of his conscience? Or was it the deep hatred that only a coward can summon up against people he hasn't the courage to face on his own? Maybe what Jamaal celebrated with every bite paid for by ill-gotten wealth was the defilement of a society that he could never challenge, where he was only a bit player, and whose accolades he could never win. Maybe what Khalid and Jamaal toasted with each cup of tea was their own defeat.

Whatever it was, it didn't suit Jamaal. Whenever he shared something to eat with Khalid his stomach would give out and he would spend half a day painfully emptying his bowels, his stomach aching and his shit coming out in a spray of loose matter and fluids. It didn't matter what it was that he ate. Whether it was a samosa or a gulab jamun, whether it was cooked at the cafeteria or came wrapped up as a piece of chocolate, his digestion could process none of it. But he never refused. Never in all the years at St Jude's, where Khalid had another four and a half years to spend, all the time becoming visibly richer as he acquired one small status symbol after another, did Jamaal refuse to eat with Khalid. But after that, during the one year that he endured St Jude's alone, his stomach ran smoothly, with never a hitch.

It was the unexpected relief that decided him. He needed to talk to somebody, and Malauna Qayoom could be found at the mosque. His father would be there as well, but Jamaal had stopped speaking of troubling or important things to Rafiq a long time ago.

It had started with the pen. Jamaal never spoke of it to his father, and when his grades deteriorated in school Rafiq tried to probe a few times before giving up in the face of Jamaal's silent obduracy.

Besides, Rafiq, increasingly, had little time to spare. He was much in demand. Manoj Tripathi, the head priest of the Hanuman mandir, had won a bitter contest to become mayor of the town. He had spent one term consolidating his hold, and then had started to broaden his campaign. As mayor he had power to influence municipal projects, especially their names. After years of trying, he had accepted that the campaign to rename the town from Moazammabad to Methi was perhaps too ambitious, but he was able to sanction the repainting of street and neighbourhood signs. And he made good use of this limited privilege. Urdu Bazaar became Hindi Bazaar, Inayat Gali was renamed Lakshman Path and the residents of Ali Nagar found that they were now living in Arya Nagar. Anything with a

Muslim name was slowly hidden and defaced, and almost every temple began, overnight, to use more powerful loudspeakers.

Not to be outdone, the mosques too bought more expensive loudspeakers, until chants and calls to prayer could be heard at all hours of the day, and much of the night. At the incredible decibels that they were being broadcast, words and languages seemed to blur, Sanskrit losing its classic austerity, merging into the languid, stretched-out vowels of Arabic. Without warning, the police swept down, and all the equipment was confiscated. But the temples received some of it back. The petitions from the mosques were piled up, and ignored.

They had broken the law.

Such times made unexpected space for Rafiq. Maybe it was only because his few dark statements had turned out right. Some years ago, for example, he had warned everybody when a TV serial based on the *Ramayana* was being shown on Doordarshan.

'Don't you understand what they're doing? They are trying to make everybody a Hindu, it's a conspiracy,' he had said at the local mosque after Friday prayers.

And someone—Jamaal couldn't quite place him—had asked, 'Arre Ansari sahib, are you trying to ban believers from watching TV again?'

'It's just another form of idolatry,' Rafiq replied. 'And now they're putting their gods and their idols on it.'

Maulana Qayoom was there, and he took the simple position that if it offended people they shouldn't watch the programme. He didn't have a TV himself.

But millions of others across the country did—in Moazammabad the main Hanuman temple put up three television sets for the devout, sponsored by the mayor. And not too far away, in Delhi, an ageing politician had an idea to make an attempt at the fame and power that had eluded him for long. You know the story, of course—though you'll be surprised how many have forgotten, or how many young people have never been told. And that's a useful thing to remember—nothing, in the end, will matter. Justice is overrated, don't you think ... But I digress again.

So this mousy-looking politician decided to ride a decorated, air-conditioned Toyota truck, as you remember, calling it a rath, that favoured vehicle of the god and king Lord Rama. He decided to make proper men of the Hindus by teaching them to be angry and to hate. And he drove his chariot along a track of blood and tears across the country to tear down a mosque so that a temple to Rama could be built upon its debris.

Riots had followed, and became regular after that, the dead piling up. A Hindu party came to power in Delhi— even if for only a fortnight, it was there. Every few months a young man, a Muslim, would be shot by the police in an encounter—that overused word suggesting almost an accidental intimacy!

And this was how Rafiq, who had warned against the serial, who had spoken of a Hindu conspiracy, came to be seen as a dark prophet, and somebody to listen to.

It is no surprise then that the topic of discussion after Friday prayers ever since has inevitably been the state of

Muslims in India. This is how it is now—you will see it everywhere, as indeed you will at the mosque here, in Rasoolpur. And this is how it was when Jamaal, in his final year at school, without Khalid's friendship but thinking only of the nature of that friendship, thought of speaking to Maulana Qayoom.

That Friday, after everybody had had their say, Jamaal asked quietly, 'Maulana sahib, what does Islam say about breaking the law?'

'Why, they should be punished of course,' one of the others said, but the imam raised his hand.

'I think you mean something different, don't you, Jamaal?' the imam said.

Jamaal wasn't used to so many people staring at him as he spoke, and he stumbled over his words. 'Umm ... I mean, how should we treat them? Not the authorities. I mean ... us? Can you still regard somebody well even if he is a criminal?'

It was an odd question, and Jamaal could feel everybody's eyes on him, especially Rafiq's. So many years had gone by since they had spoken of things other than routine matters, but Rafiq was still Jamaal's father, he knew that his son was speaking of a matter other than what he asked. Maybe that was why he kept uncharacteristically quiet, letting the Maulana speak uninterrupted.

'In his collection of Hadith, Imam Bukhari records that Anas stated that the Prophet, peace be upon Him, said, "Help your brother, whether he is an oppressor or is oppressed." When people asked, "O Allah's apostle, it is all right to help him if he is oppressed, but how should we help him if he is an oppressor?" The Prophet, peace be upon Him, said, "By preventing him from oppressing others."'

'But what if the people he is oppressing are oppressors themselves?' Jamaal asked.

'Yes, Maulana sahib, what if a criminal is acting against greater criminals?' one of the older men there repeated Jamaal's question. 'Look at Dawood Ibrahim. He's a criminal, and he killed many innocents by those blasts in Bombay, but he stopped the riots there, didn't he?'

Suddenly everybody was talking, and the question that Jamaal had mustered the courage to ask after so long was lost in a deluge of other queries.

'To kill innocents is a crime,' the imam said. 'Islam forbids any attack on non-combatants.'

'But what if the whole of society is against you?' somebody wanted to know.

'All of Mecca was against God's apostle, peace be upon Him,' the imam answered, 'but he did not resort to attacks on the entire city.'

'Maulana sahib,' Jamaal tried again, 'but if you can only bring the smaller criminal to justice, and it means that the bigger oppressors get away with oppression, aren't you aiding them in oppression?'

Maulana Qayoom was patient with him; he had seen the boy grow up before him, always a little quieter and more serious than the others. 'It is forbidden to wage war except within the rules that God has set for us, beta. Justice will be done by God alone. We must do what we can according to His law.'

'So we should suffer, and even hand our own people over to the police?' one of the men said. 'That makes no sense.'

Rafiq spoke then, unable to keep silent any longer. 'Our religion forbids us aiding oppression, even by voluntarily submitting to it.'

It was an odd phrase. He didn't contradict the imam, but the way he said it, the bitter undertone, meant something very different from what the imam was saying. Jamaal looked at his father, at the taut expression on his face, and realized that he could never tell anybody the truth about Khalid. Least of all his father.

13

Jamaal's testimony turned out to be unnecessary in the end. They caught Khalid red-handed by the railway station, trying to sell a stolen motorcycle. They would have caught his partner as well, but he disappeared. Or maybe he knew not to turn up. Or maybe, as some rumours had it, the police did catch Khalid's partner but money and influence oiled the hands of the law and he managed to slip free, leaving only Khalid behind, Khalid the bastard, whose father had neither the wealth nor the influence to keep his son from jail.

The arrest sent shockwaves through the town. However poor or despicable his father might be, Khalid was also the nephew of Ahmad Saeed Shabbir who, after his father passed away three years ago, had become president of the Waqf Board, managing all the properties kept in trust by the Muslims, and their unofficial leader. The shame was immense, and somewhere beneath it all was the fear that if the police could put Ahmad Saeed's nephew in jail, then no Muslim was safe.

It wasn't a matter of criminality. Didn't everybody know

that Dilip Aggarwal, the son of the owner of the fertilizer plant, had shot and killed his wife, even if the police would never file a case? Hadn't other deaths too been hushed up, rapes as well, and all manner of crimes committed by people of all religions and all kinds, whether politician or policeman, businessman or judge, as long as the criminal was of a certain class, with a family that had deep pockets? Why was Khalid in jail now? And could it be only a coincidence that the mosque had been torn down only a few years ago, and that the Bombay bomb blasts were still talked about as if they had happened not some years but a few days ago?

For reasons known only to himself, Ahmad Saeed hesitated. Perhaps despite his position he was never fully comfortable being the leader of the town's Muslims alone. Maybe he had reason to believe that Khalid really was a criminal and there was no use petitioning the government on his behalf. Or maybe he was just scared.

Elections for the mayor of the city were only a few weeks away, and as always there were only two serious contestants ringed by a crowd of non-entities. By tradition the seat of the mayor passed between the head of the Talwalkar family and Manoj Tripathi, the second son of the Tripathi household, who was also the head priest at the Hanuman mandir. There would be very little campaigning, the candidates simply coming to meet the head of every major neighbourhood to canvass for their support.

There were no direct elections, of course. It was the corporators, chosen from each area by the people, who in turn elected the mayor. Fully a third of the twenty-six corporators in Moazzamabad were elected from Muslim localities, and for this reason the support of the Shabbirs, the most important Muslim family in the city, was invaluable. Everyone who aspired to be mayor of Moazzamabad knew and accepted this. Except Manoj Tripathi.

Even the first time he stood for mayor, Tripathi had already decided to break with tradition. He hadn't come to meet Ahmad Saeed, nor had he visited any Muslim locality for support. The omission hadn't harmed him in any way; he had won the election. The mosque in Ayodhya was demolished during his first term as mayor, and he had distributed sweets at the Hanuman temple in celebration. It was also whispered that he had promised that every mosque, even the one in Rasoolpur, would soon be destroyed to make way for a temple.

Now, it was Tripathi's fourth attempt to become mayor, and though by tradition a Talwalkar should have occupied the office, everyone knew that times had changed. It was said that Rajiv Talwalkar was rethinking his decision to contest. He had come to Rasoolpur, and Ahmad Saeed had assured him of the vote from the corporators he could influence, but Talwalkar appeared to have conceded defeat already. Everyone in Rasoolpur was talking about a secret pact between Tripathi and Talwalkar, some even suggesting that what lay behind the pact was more threat than inducement.

Perhaps this uncertainty, this sign of times changing and

Shabbir Manzil losing its position of influence, was why
Ahmad Saeed hesitated. He didn't go to the jail until two
days after Khalid's arrest, by which time, in any case, the
pressure of public curiosity had become unbearable and he
couldn't show his face in the mohalla for shame. When he
finally got into the jeep, the only person to accompany him
was the tall, cadaverous figure of Waris Ahmed, a man
who had served as the clerk of the elder Shabbir sahib,
Ahmad Saeed's father, and was credited with knowing
more points of law than the combined bar association of
Moazzamabad. In his hands was a sheaf of papers, held
together in the typical brown folder with a ribbon,
proclaiming that they were legal notices.

Bail, it was whispered, and then everybody realized how
foolish they had been. Ahmad Saeed had to arrange the
bail—what would have been the point of going to see the
boy if he couldn't free him?

If only Ahmad Saeed had known that there *was* a point
in visiting the jail immediately, if he had just cared more,
or been less nervous about going to the police station
without legal cover—maybe then it could all have been
averted. But how was Ahmad Saeed to know that they
would start beating the boy so soon, and so savagely? He
could not possibly have imagined that the police would
bring out a man stinking of urine, shuffling along on the
bruised soles of his feet, with a cut lip and torn clothes,
and tell him that this was his, Ahmad Saeed Shabbir's,
nephew.

'Khalid?' Ahmad Saeed said in surprise, and the battered

boy raised his head, and looked at him with eyes that still held something of their mulish stubbornness. Then he opened his mouth to speak, and Ahmad Saeed was appalled to see the space left behind by a broken tooth. Khalid simply whispered, 'Badeabba . . .'

'What have you done to him?' Ahmad Saeed exclaimed.

The Station House Officer, an inspector nattily dressed in a crisply ironed uniform said, 'He attacked my men. What do you expect?'

Khalid no longer had to struggle to find his voice. 'Liar,' he said. 'Why don't you just admit that you beat me because I'm a Muslim?'

Inspector Rawat pointed the shiny end of his baton at him and said, 'Why you lying little thief . . .'

'What thief?' Khalid asked. 'What proof do you have except a confession that you beat out of me?'

'Is this true?' Waris Ahmed asked before the inspector could refute him.

'Of course it isn't,' the inspector replied in frustration. 'We caught him red-handed just about to sell the motorcycle.'

'To whom?' Waris Ahmed asked. 'I don't see another prisoner. Where is the buyer?'

Inspector Rawat had an answer, but he couldn't give it. So he decided to say nothing.

'You had better have a good case,' Waris Ahmed said. 'And some very good witnesses to say that your men acted in self-defence when they beat up this boy.'

This was too much for the inspector. 'Or what?' he

asked. 'What will you do? The boy is a thief. We caught him, and he confessed. We have the details of a dozen robberies that he committed in the last six months, and he squealed like a pig the last two days in prison, told us everything.'

'You had better have a good case,' Waris Ahmed repeated, unfazed, and then turned to follow Ahmad Saeed as the older man helped his nephew out of jail.

At the Suleiman Medical Centre, as the doctor washed the cuts, applied balm, and put Khalid through a battery of tests, Waris Ahmed told Ahmad Saeed that the case was weak. Unless the police presented the buyer, a confession was just not enough, even if they did recover the stolen goods. There was little chance that they could successfully prosecute such a case, especially in the light of the beating the boy had endured.

When the doctor brought Khalid out, telling Ahmad Saeed that they would have to wait for the results but it seemed that there was no permanent damage except a badly chipped tooth, Ahmad Saeed told Khalid that the police had no case, even with the stolen goods.

'What stolen goods?' Khalid asked, his eyes flat and malevolent. 'I'm no thief. They just stopped me on the street and asked me my name. When I told them, they asked me if I would come along with them to identify my friend Raghav's motorcycle that had been stolen two days ago, and took me in their jeep to the forest. The motorcycle was lying flat on the ground, and its licence plate had been removed. When I pushed it upright, I recognized the sticker that Raghav had stuck on the side of the fuel tank. "So you can tell it's stolen," the inspector said to me. "I bet you know a lot about stolen goods." When I asked him what he meant, he said he had a lot to discuss with me, and they took me to jail.'

He paused before continuing. 'And then they started beating me, and abusing me, telling me that I was a bastard, a thief, a motherfucking Muslim, and on and on, for hours. When I passed out, they threw water on me, and then started beating me again. They tied me down to a table and beat the soles of my feet. They wouldn't even let me go to the toilet, just made me piss on myself, and then they continued to beat me until I said I'd say whatever they wanted me to say, do whatever they wanted me to do, just so that they'd stop. They made me write out a confession. And then you came.'

Ahmad Saeed was stunned. He had never heard something like this before. It was like in a movie. Even the doctor standing next to Khalid was moved by the power of the story. Only Waris Ahmad thought that it sounded too good, almost rehearsed, without a word out of place, and that the police inspector would have dictated a confession only if he had collected the stolen goods beforehand. But all he said was, 'I've told the inspector he should have a very good case.'

'He won't,' Khalid replied. He had a small grin on his face and Waris Ahmed thought to himself that sometimes it wasn't enough to be a thief. The best of thieves needed to be liars as well, and such good liars that even the most experienced of men, even hardened policemen, would think that they had managed to get their hands on the truth, only to come away empty-handed.

The story of Khalid's torture at the hands of the police reached everybody in Rasoolpur mohalla by that afternoon. There were many who could recite, word for word, what Khalid had said about his experience, and there were many more who retold the story using their own imagination, adding electric shocks, acid and sodomy to the mix. Half a day more, and the spine-chilling news was being told and heard all over Moazzamabad, even beyond.

By that time Inspector Rawat too had understood that a thief could be a liar as well, and a good one, good enough to fool Rawat, maybe good enough to destroy his career. He called Manoj Tripathi's office, and was told that the priest and two-time mayor would see him at half past five, and that Rawat should come and say his prayers at the temple.

'Give me Haria,' Rawat said, as he sat before the priest that evening. But Tripathi didn't reply.

'I need Haria,' Rawat repeated. 'You said that he was your man, that you needed him, and that the boy would talk. I need Haria to make the case.'

'What happened?' Tripathi finally asked.

'The boy talked all right, but he lied. He made fools out of us. We thought he was confessing, but he gave us nothing. All the locations are false. The goods are somewhere else.'

'Haria can tell you where they are.'

'No,' Rawat said, shaking his head. 'No. Haria told me that the boy never revealed where he stashed the material. And anyway, even if I can recover the goods, he's chosen such locations in the confession that he could easily prove that we didn't find them there. One of them is the house of a sitting high court judge! The minute we produce that confession the case will be thrown out of court. If the press get their hands on it nobody will be able to save me.'

'He made a fool out of you, and you want my man?'

'Look, if Haria confesses, in court, and identifies the boy, I'll make sure he gets a milder sentence. With any luck he'll be out of jail in six months.'

Tripathi said nothing for a moment, thinking, and then asked, 'You think that Haria's confession would prove anything?'

'At least it would prove that I didn't cook up the case,' Rawat said desperately. 'Otherwise, not only will I lose my job, I could even end up in jail.'

The policeman's fear made the priest break into laughter. 'Don't worry,' he said. 'You don't know Moazzamabad. And you don't know how to deal with these Mussalmans. It's just the boy, isn't it? Don't you know that he's a bastard? Haven't you realized that not even his father spoke up for him? It took two days for them to come and fetch him from jail. Get rid of him and you'll be doing them a favour. They'll thank you soon enough, but only after you've done their dirty work for them. Useless sons of whores don't even know how to get rid of their own criminals; we have to do it for them.'

Rawat shook his head. 'I can't do anything right now.'
The priest smiled. 'Let me show you how it's done.'

Two days later the men came for Khalid. It was at the medical centre. There were three of them having tea, and a driver in the jeep. They had been waiting all day, from ten in the morning—for their elderly aunt, they said, who was expected anytime. But it was at the sight of Khalid in the rickshaw that they sprang to attention. He was still walking with crutches, and as he descended from the rickshaw, slow and tentative, the men put away their teacups and started to walk purposefully towards him.

People casually made way for them, as they unthinkingly do when larger men move in a particular manner towards their goal. They would have probably gotten away with it, except that at the last minute, just as one of them was about to reach out to grab Khalid's arm, Khalid seemed to slip. The man stretched his arm farther to catch the falling boy, but Khalid was not falling, and at nineteen years of age he was no longer just a boy. His elbow came up hard, and made a sickening noise as it sank into the man's exposed neck, into his Adam's apple. As the first man fell, choking, Khalid whirled around, dropping one crutch, holding the other with both hands like a cricket bat, and drove it with all his strength into the side of the second man's head.

And suddenly the third man was left all alone—one of his companions lay unconscious, with a bleeding scalp, and the other was gasping helplessly for breath on the ground.

'Come on, motherfucker,' Khalid yelled.

The man didn't have such courage. He'd never hunted alone. He turned to flee, but now the people didn't make way for him. They knew Khalid, and they knew his story. He might not have been a hero in Rasoolpur, but he was one of them, and close to being a martyr. They wouldn't allow some thugs to kidnap him from under their noses, now that they understood who these men were, or at least what they had been attempting to do.

The driver saw the crowd start to beat the third man, and made a fatal mistake. He had been ready to go, but in his hurry he pressed too hard on the accelerator just as the jeep roared into life—and the engine choked into silence. He had been driving the jeep for years, and he should have remembered that the engine had a tendency to flood, but fear had overwhelmed him. Soon the crowd overwhelmed him as well, pulling him out, beating him down, and then, just as he lost consciousness, he saw that somebody had set fire to the jeep. His last emotion was terror. It was a petrol jeep, chosen for its quick acceleration so they could make a clean getaway, and unlike diesel petrol doesn't merely burn, it explodes.

14

Should Jamaal have spoken then? If people knew exactly what kind of person Khalid was, would the fires have burnt that bright, or for so long? Who can tell?

And maybe in all that I am telling you there is nothing to help us make sense of this town, our mohalla, that boy. We understand so little, after all . . .

But let me finish my story nevertheless.

So Jamaal told no one. He watched, he listened. Most of all to his father.

Rafiq was at the forefront of things, but in an odd way. He was not involved in violence, God forbid the thought, nor did he make speeches or lead demonstrations. No, what he did instead was to present facts. Perhaps because he was a teacher, he had a way of saying things, of recalling an incident, so that a fact was no longer just a fact but a lesson, the wisdom of history. As Khalid's story whirled through the mohalla, Rafiq recalled for people the recent incident of two Muslim boys going missing from the railway station in Lucknow, and their bodies turning up mysteriously in the Gomti river three days later. He recalled, too, that a journalist—a Sikh—had started digging around for details of the boys' disappearance, and one day his car was hit by a police truck whose brakes had failed. The journalist had survived, but his investigations had not.

Rafiq knew dozens of such facts, collected from newspapers and committed to memory so that he could tell them as stories of their time to those of his neighbourhood who cared to listen. People congregated to hear him now, as tension gripped the mohalla. They arrived at his house as they had once turned up at Shabbir Manzil. The only difference was that no one was turned away from Rafiq's.

Initially Jamaal stayed, making tea and listening, adding nothing of his own. To say what he knew of Khalid would be inappropriate in these gatherings; it might even be seen as treacherous. He couldn't risk that. But there were times when he wanted to stop them and say, 'Look, this isn't an innocent you are talking about. This is Khalid the thief.'

But he had never spoken before, and how could he speak now? He had never trained for it, he had no experience, nor even any great desire to speak his mind. How could he correct his father when he had never told him the truth about the broken pen, or about the reason why his stomach had reacted badly to the things Khalid fed him?

Rafiq, on the other hand, had spent a lifetime waiting to hold forth. He had practiced silently to himself all those long years in near obscurity. Stories flowed out of him now. Jamaal had never seen his father like this. Rafiq had always been the man who said odd things, briefly, abruptly—dark words that everybody thought of but would not speak. The fact that he would say these unspeakable things had found him a place, but that place was on the sidelines. Now, though, the end of the world was approaching. They had ignored it for so long, and they had been wrong. Rafiq, it seemed, had been the only one willing to look truth in the face. People clustered around him, as they had never done before, for whatever it was that he could offer.

Alone with his story, the wrong story that was locked inside his head like an urgent secret, Jamaal could think of little else. And every day he thought about it, it became more wrong, not less. After all, what did it matter if Khalid was a thief? There were other thieves, and were they beaten as he had been? Nobody had tried to kidnap or kill them in broad daylight. If they were looking to kill Khalid, then, was it because he was a thief or because he was a Muslim? All Jamaal had to do was listen to his father, to see the peace on his father's face when he recalled another violent or hushed-up incident, from another time, and showed how it all fit. This was how it was all connected, and even if the end of the world was coming, he seemed to be saying, at least they were not sheep that they would go to their deaths without knowledge, without recognizing the true face of their executioners. The crime they had committed was to be Muslim, nothing more, nothing less.

It wasn't because he was a thief that Khalid had been tortured and kidnapped. And it wasn't the reason why dozens, hundreds, thousands, might now die.

There was only one person that Jamaal could turn to, for

solace and clarity, but he struggled with the decision, did not know whether he should speak. The mosque, in any case, was no longer a place where people would gather as they did before. There were always policemen there. And what would he tell Maulana Qayoom, what would the imam hear? And anyway, were his questions so important? So he hesitated, and he hesitated too long.

After the day that Manoj Tripathi's men had come for Khalid and failed, curfew days finally reached Moazzamabad. But not immediately. That evening, that week, was odd. Very few things changed in reality, but it was as if there was a difference in the humidity and temperature, in the air they breathed. The mohalla was both energized and curiously reluctant to do anything. All things seemed to be possible, but nobody really did much except talk. It was what revolutions must feel like. The police had disappeared, and one after another people looked up and around. There was a sense, a suspicion, that everything that they took for granted, the rules and orders of everyday life, were unnecessary. Or—no, that was not strictly true. What they realized was that the only people keeping them in their cage were themselves, and this thought both freed and paralysed them. Freedom of course is the great temptation—the great, fatal temptation, wouldn't you agree?—and it was tempting here too, then as it is now. But there was also fear—of being free, of what would happen the day after freedom.

It should have been the ideal time for the people who

hated the state to rise up, except that they needed a state to hate. The police weren't around for them to revolt against, and for a while Rafiq found himself with a diminished audience. If there was freedom to be had, why should he be listened to, why should anyone be listened to?

And then the police were back, in force. No one had seen so many, nor of the kind who arrived.

Curfew was declared. Pickets were set up at the major crossroads in town, but this was a mohalla so there were only minor crossroads. A large truck painted in camouflage trundled up close to Shabbir Manzil and disgorged its contents. These were no ordinary police, even their khaki was different, and they were armed with submachine guns. The street shook a little when they jumped out, a stream of young and middle-aged men with surprisingly clean boots.

The people of the mohalla, like stunned cattle, found themselves herded into their homes, the peace enforced by the threat of gunfire. That was when the resistance rose, and speeches were made. But they were only made in the safety of the home, and sometimes in the mosque. This was Rasoolpur after all, resistance did not mean picking up a gun. The greatest violence we knew was that of a cutting remark.

But the world was bigger than Rasoolpur; Moazzamabad was bigger than Rasoolpur, and the world was so much bigger even than Moazzamabad. The world crept in, almost by stealth. Slowly things that we had only heard about—things that were happening in the rest of the country—

began to happen in our town. In small ways. The muezzins set their loudspeakers in the mosques a little louder, or maybe they just sounded that way in the new situation. The chants and bhajans from the temples sounded louder as well. At some point of time, it was difficult to tell exactly when, there were more insistent calls to prayer being sent out from our mosque early in the morning, and the chants from the temples around our neighbourhood began to reach us earlier and earlier in the morning.

To those cooped up in their homes the war to be the loudest began like this, until there was only the noise of aggression, no call to God at all left in the way that people were summoned to state their loyalties.

In that compressed and wound-up space rumours spread, first like stains and then like small fires. Somebody had been killed by the police, a priest had been caught with guns in his Maruti van, a young woman had been raped—always such women were beautiful, and then ritually slashed and scarred. Always the mob was coming to kill.

All of this had happened before, but it took on an added edge now. Jamaal was a teenager when the curfew days began. He learned that curfew fear was of a different quality and texture than any other he had encountered. Sitting in his house, he saw the fear not only in his own face when he looked in the mirror, but caught it on his father's face as well. He could see the mark it left, a yellowing and tautness of the skin that was unmistakable. And he could see it in the twitching of the eyes that would always look away after brief contract.

It was a virus in the gut, spreading silently in the blood, infecting the heart and the mind. Maybe it really was a sickness that had been identified and recorded in medical books long ago, and a good doctor could detect it as infallibly as malaria. Jamaal wasn't sure, he didn't know, and after a while he wondered if it was only he who was looking for signs of curfew sickness.

Or maybe it was just that everyone was sick in those days, and who wanted to be reminded of their own failing health? In the constricted hours, curfew fear sat crouched in Rafiq and Jamaal's living room, feeding on slips of the tongue and growing more massive by the hour.

During the hours when the curfew was lifted there was a strange feeling of carnival, as if everyone wanted to talk at once. Funnily enough, they would congregate at Rafiq's house, and listen to him talk about fear instead, about being hunted, about the end of the world. It seemed to relax Rafiq somehow, as if their greater fear mitigated his own illness and made him healthy. Or perhaps what helped him was the simple fact that people listened to him. Now, after all those years of obscurity and frustration.

For Jamaal it was unbearable, to be freed from fear for some hours, only to be subjected to even greater fears. He would run away from the house, with the excuse of groceries to be bought, little household errands to be done. But on his return there was nothing else to do, except to share the enclosed space with Rafiq who had the shiny-eyed look, those days, of a doomsday prophet.

Where could Jamaal run from that—when he was jailed

within his own house, where could he escape? When his own father seemed to thrive off the dangers of the time, Jamaal's cowardice overwhelmed him. The fear became an invisible, obsequious, unshakeable pet, like a mangy street dog that had adopted him, whose sweat grew rancid and soaked into every small part of his life. The stink of it was in every piece of clothing he wore. Even when the curfew was finally lifted and he walked out of the house without thought of where he shouldn't go and when he should scuttle back indoors, he carried the stench in his clothes.

The worst of it was that the fear was not unreasonable. All that Rafiq said made perfect sense.

When the whole country was burning it seemed impossible that any town or city, any person, should remain untouched. More than once the news had come, whispered or spoken out loud in anger or alarm, telling them the mob was already on its way to gut and burn their mohalla and slaughter everyone who lived there. Always it had turned out to be a mere rumour, but they could never be sure when it would be the real thing. Did they not already know, wasn't Rafiq there to remind them, that the khaki of the police was the uniform of callous disregard, if not hate? Didn't they know well that the law could be a cliff that they could batter their hands to pulp against, and still it would give them no shelter?

It did something to Jamaal, that knowledge, the reasonableness with which Rafiq explained it all. Jamaal understood. He was sure he understood. When he heard the news now, he knew exactly which mohalla the mob had set out from—he knew because his schoolmates lived there. He knew that they would be part of the maddened hundred-armed creature carrying axes, iron rods, tridents and kerosene cans that would break down the door looking for him and his father. One night, he woke with a start, shivering with dread and cowered under his bed, till shame forced him to crawl out. That marked him—the shame. And the absolute loneliness, for nothing isolates you as completely as the thought of dying.

There is something obscene in being eighteen years old and knowing the face of your death so well that you can draw in the details. You see that face when your classmate refuses to meet your eye and you wonder if he's thinking about your murder.

Jamaal learnt a lot in those days, through his last year at St Jude's.

He bloated up with the knowledge. And this knowledge had the smell and taste and feel of fear. Although outwardly he was thin to the point of being skeletal, he felt obese with his fear as it grew a little every hour, till it was straining the insides of his skin. Had his father not been there, Jamaal would have flung himself out onto those eerily empty roads, towards the guns of the policemen keeping the peace. He would have died there, and it would have been the end of it all.

One night he almost did it; the whole mohalla almost did. It was after a week when the curfew had been enforced rigorously, only a couple of hours allowed in the morning and the evening for people to scurry to the stores for supplies and return, panting, to their prisons. That evening had been no different from the others, unnaturally silent, people recovering from the quickened pulse and tension of the two-hour reprieve. And then the chanting started. It was so loud that it would have needed countless hundreds to make such a sound, a veritable army.

It began as a slow rumble just before midnight, and grew into a roar within minutes. You could hear the hate, the religious frenzy of the mob that was coming, and everybody in Rasoolpur knew that they were going to be killed. The police and paramilitary would stand aside to let the terrifying mob in this time, and nobody would escape.

There was no point in staying inside, and people sneaked out slowly to their balconies to look out into the darkness, to see the shape of their death. But there was nothing to see. The sound was coming from across the wide sewer line and there were no lights there. The only movement was that of the policemen and soldiers stationed in their trucks, and they seemed to be cowering at the unexpected attack.

Suddenly Bashir Qasim appeared at the gate of his house. A middle-aged man, he was dressed in a white kurta-pyjama. In his hand was the sword that had been preserved in his family for centuries. Since all the guns in the neighbourhood had been confiscated at the beginning of the curfew, this was all he could find to defend himself. Always a bit portly, Bashir Qasim looked strangely thin and fragile in the yellow of the sodium lights. As the men in uniform hid, and the neighbourhood cowered, Bashir Qasim raised the sword and roared the old war cry back at the hidden mob: '*Naar e takbeer, Allah u Akbar!*'

His voice cracked at the first attempt, but then he roared again, challenging the killers advancing towards his home. And then, one by one, other people took up the cry and in minutes the residents of the neighbourhood were out in the streets, armed with kitchen knives and roaring, again and again, '*Naar e takbeer, Allah u Akbar!*'

It was then that the men in uniform sprang to attention. Jeeps and trucks with flashing lights and sirens drove into the streets of Rasoolpur, scattering people in pyjamas out of their way. Within fifteen minutes the mohalla was covered with men in khaki, and then abruptly the sound of the threatening mob vanished. It was only the next day that people found out that there had been no mob, just three tape recorders fixed to loudspeakers placed strategically across from Rasoolpur and turned on full at the dead of night.

Bashir Qasim's sword was confiscated. Everybody knew that it was Manoj Tripathi who had arranged the trick with the loudspeakers, but nothing could be proved. What could easily be proved was that the police were not there to protect the residents of Rasoolpur, but to strip them of all their defences instead.

The next day, as Jamaal was slicing onions for salad to go with the dinner, an idea came to him.

No. It wasn't quite like that. There was no thinking. He just washed the knife, dried it, and his right hand slipped it in the gap between the rolled up sleeve and the skin of his upper left arm. It took a second for the cold metal to warm next to his skin, and Jamaal rolled the sleeve a little tighter to hold the knife, but it fit almost naturally.

It is impossible to recall how many times the fear came and passed. You do not count the day of your death; it is only supposed to happen once. You remember the old cliché that a brave man dies only the one death while a coward dies many, many times? Maybe Jamaal was a coward then, and he died many times. But not, as they say, in reality. The mob that was always coming for us never actually arrived, and the Police Armed Constabulary, the PAC, somehow never made it to our door collecting men and boys for target practice.

After the horror of those weeks, Jamaal found himself, strangely enough, still alive.

When a dog bites a man, the man learns to fear. When a dog slavers, barks and howls at the sight of a man, when it chases him down the street and corners him against a wall and is then unexpectedly called back by its owner, what does the man learn?

15

The curfew ended, but it stunted many lives. Like Jamaal's. The fear and confusion extended well beyond those powder-keg days, and there came a time when Jamaal found that he had done little to secure his future. Maybe somewhere in the world you can find a job when all you have is a modicum of ambition, a bachelor's degree in history and the ability to hide a kitchen knife on your person without letting it show. Not in Moazzamabad.

Jamaal even missed the tech revolution. He did not study computers, but he was taught typing on broken-down machines in the college, the only boy among a roomful of girls who hid their smiles behind their hands and giggled at him. And what was a computer in Moazzamabad anyway but a glorified typewriter? When the opportunity came, Jamaal was ready to be a typist.

As the memory of curfew and violence faded, few people came to listen to Rafiq. They had less time, less patience, too. They even had opinions of their own that Rafiq had to listen to, silent against his will. One evening when Jamaal returned from his college he found Rafiq sitting alone at home.

'As salaam aleikum Abba,' he said.

Rafiq looked up at him, but took a while to reply. 'Wa aleikum as salaam.'

The pause had been just long enough for Jamaal to hesitate. He could not go into his room now; so he asked, 'Would you like some tea?'

'No son, I've had tea.'

As Jamaal stood, unsure, Rafiq said, 'You asked once, at the mosque, whether it is right for a thief to steal from a tyrant.'

That wasn't exactly what Jamaal had asked, and it had been a long time ago, but he nodded.

'Did you ever get an answer?'

Jamaal almost blurted out, 'No, you didn't allow it.' But he just shook his head.

'I've been thinking about it,' Rafiq said, 'for years. For decades.'

Jamaal still had no words to offer, none to risk, and it seemed that Rafiq, too, wasn't interested in any. He closed his eyes, and appeared to fall asleep, the muscles of his face rearranging themselves so that Jamaal could see the roundness of his father's natural features, marked by the lines that came of keeping them deliberately hard and still for long years.

'I don't know if there is an answer,' Rafiq said finally, so softly that Jamaal could barely hear him.

Then his voice took on strength, although he kept his eyes tightly closed. 'No. I'm sorry, there is an answer. A clear and unambiguous one. It is wrong. The thief should be caught, condemned. But I don't know if we have the strength to do that, not in a society where the tyrant rules. Maybe that is why tyranny is so cruel. It does not take away our knowledge of what we must do, just our strength to do so.'

Jamaal's face flushed and he could hear the sudden hammering of the blood in his veins. He could not believe that his father knew. That Khalid's crimes had been discovered, and his own silence as well.

Then Rafiq opened his eyes, and Jamaal realized that Rafiq did not know. Or even if he did, this was not what he was talking about. His gaze was focused elsewhere, somewhere far away, or maybe far inside of him; either way, it was a place where Jamaal could not go, and where Khalid did not exist.

'Where you cannot live by your faith, there you must fight for it, or if you have not the strength, flee,' Rafiq said, quoting the Hadith, the sayings of the Prophet. Jamaal had heard him quote them before, but always with fire and stone in his voice, not like this, not gently, in defeat, even in a kind of compassion.

'What are you going to do after college?' Rafiq asked.

The question was so unexpected that Jamaal answered without thinking. 'I will do an MBA. I'll give the Common Admission Test for the IIMs.'

Rafiq leaned back and looked at Jamaal uncertainly, blinking as if he was surprised to see him there. 'Institutes of Management? They're difficult to get into.'

'Yes. But I can study hard,' Jamaal replied.

'Not the civil service exams?' Rafiq asked. Those too were incredibly difficult, so Jamaal wondered a little at the question.

'No,' he said. And he knew that he did not need to explain to his father, of all people, why he did not wish to be part of the government, to wear khaki as a police officer, or drive in a car with a whirling blue light and siren. He did not want to be part of all that. He would take the CAT exam, would study hard, maybe even go to the tuition centres that were springing up. An MBA from an IIM guaranteed a salary that would allow him to live like a king. Or maybe, as his father said, to flee.

'It would be good discipline if you had a job as well, while you study for those exams,' Rafiq said.

Jamaal nodded, not caring, lost in dreams.

So Rafiq found the perfect arrangement for Jamaal: a part-time job as a typist in a shop that needed someone whose English was good enough to compose letters for all those endlessly applying for jobs, benefits, favours and a thousand other things that sustained them but were so hard to come by. The owner, Kamaal sahib, had been a classmate of Rafiq's many years ago at St Jude's, and the old connection still worked. Everybody took it for granted that Jamaal would only work there for a bit, until he made it through the MBA entrance exam. There were a few thousand others in the town also striving towards the same goal, but he was from St Jude's, and there was more hope from him than from the others. Some days, the dream of a future kingly salary glowed off Jamaal like a soft, warm light.

Jamaal was a bit of a dreamer, had always been, and that was what made him such a good typist on Kamaal sahib's newly acquired computer. The little shop did good business with him there, and he even suggested a few words for lovers writing paeans of praise to their sweethearts in a language that was not their own. English in our parts is a mark of privilege, after all, and a potential lover always aspires to sophistication. Jamaal had read many poems as part of his English literature classes, and he plagiarized shamelessly. Keats and Byron would have been as bemused by the potential lovers as the lovers themselves were by the words that Jamaal suggested.

The mood of love affected Jamaal too. He didn't lose his heart, but he began to ready himself for its consequences. He printed out, in bold letters, lines from one of his favourite poems by Yeats and put them up on the wall above his desk: 'Never give all the heart, for love/ Will hardly seem worth thinking of/ To passionate women if it seem/ Certain, and they never dream/ That it fades out from kiss to kiss/ For everything that's lovely is/ But a brief, dreamy, kind delight.'

All the mention of kisses and passion was a bit daring in Moazzamabad. Jamaal was lucky that it was Kamaal sahib who was his boss. A person who had studied at a school other than St Jude's might have been scandalized, but Kamaal sahib only smiled, and said, 'Oh, Yeats. I always liked him.' Jamaal often found his customers silently mouthing the words of the poem when he looked up at them as he worked on their letters.

It all seemed to work well and Kamaal sahib decided to give Jamaal a small raise after his third month at the shop.

And then they killed Maulana Qayoom.

It was a misunderstanding. Not his murder, but what led to it. A man was sitting eating his dinner at a dhaba. He was also drinking from a brown glass bottle. The bottle had a label that he could barely read, and would never be able to pronounce, but it made him slightly drunk, and that was all he cared about.

The owner of the dhaba had been staring suspiciously at the man for the last half hour, the drunk diner was not just taking his time to finish, his presence meant that many others were avoiding the place. Finally, as a wedding party approached slowly from up the street, the owner asked the man to pay and leave.

'What?' the man asked, and his hand moved suddenly. The bottle, slick with his sweat, slipped out of his hand and shattered as it fell.

Both the diner and the dhaba owner stared down at the mess at their feet.

'You broke my bottle,' the drunk said, and slapped the owner.

This was too much for the dhaba owner, and he yelled back at his son, 'Amit, get my cleaver, quick. I'm going to teach this bastard a lesson.'

The threat was only meant to inspire fear, and it succeeded beyond the dhaba owner's expectations. The drunk wailed, and spinning around, plunged headlong into the wedding party, right into the centre, where the women were dancing. He pawed and clawed as he tried to get through the sudden throng of brightly coloured celebrants.

The shrieks of the frightened women silenced the crowd, and because these were women who rarely ventured out onto the street, the fury of the men who were supposed to be guarding them was beyond description. Maybe it was also because this was a Muslim wedding party, and the Muslims of Moazzamabad had lived in fear for many years now, watching Manoj Tripathi rise from being a nobody priest, to mayor, and now a Member of the Legislative Assembly through a long, steady campaign of insult and intimidation. So, when the drunk attacked their women, their rage knew no bounds.

He was dead long before the police could get there.

And the next day, before curfew was declared, but when rumour had already sped out into the town, three of Manoj Tripathi's men spotted Maulana Qayoom walking down the road. One of them had a can of kerosene that he had been taking to the Hanuman mandir for its generator. Now the men thought it could be put to better use. They had never seen a human burn before, but they had all heard the stories: Nobody screamed louder and longer for mercy than a man on fire. So after they beat the old man to the ground, they emptied the can of kerosene over his body. He was unconscious when they poured the kerosene on him, which you would think was for the best, but it saved him only from an animal fear. He wasn't spared the pain. For, when the match fell on him and his body exploded first into a ball of blue and then into yellow-brown flames, Maulana Jalali Qayoom was brought back to his senses.

The three men watched, fascinated, as the old man's skin burned and peeled away and he screamed and screamed. And when he collapsed, they watched the flesh turn white and the fat melt and run. Then they realized that the police would be coming, and fled from the burning man. It was only later, at the temple, among their compatriots, that they claimed credit for it.

Curfew was clamped down again. In the temple they ran short of kerosene the next day, and the loudspeakers went silent during the daily power cut, but nobody there blamed the three men for the nuisance.

16

Jamaal could not attend the last prayer for Maulana Qayoom; the curfew was only relaxed three days later, and the burial had already taken place by then. Instead he went to pray at the grave. Somehow, though, words failed him. He couldn't recall the Arabic that the Maulana had taught him, and finally, out of desperation, he prayed in Urdu, a language that he could understand, and hoped God would as well.

It was a heretical thought. Just as the thought that they had made half a Hindu out of the Maulana at his death, cremating him before he was buried. The thought struck him as he made his way out of the graveyard, and he wanted to laugh, to laugh very hard indeed, but he didn't. Perhaps if he had, he would not have trembled through the day like a wound-up toy.

It isn't surprising, then, that the small incident later that day had the impact it did. A group of young men came to the shop and demanded to see the owner. Kamaal sahib came hurriedly, because that is how good men respond when faced by a group of young men in saffron bandanas wielding staffs and tridents.

Their leader said simply, 'We are collecting money for the temple.'

He did not have to mention which temple, or who they were. Everybody recognized Manoj Tripathi's men. There was only one temple whose prosperity was based on the money collected from traders and small businessmen like this owner of a typing and photocopying shop, a frightened man paying a tax to someone else's god.

Kamaal sahib was neither theologian nor lawyer. He reached into his drawer and withdrew two hundred-rupee notes, a little over twice the amount Jamaal earned in a day, and dropped it into the tin presented before him. He knew from long experience that this was just the amount that would spare him humiliation, or worse, and not wipe out his day's profit.

The leader of the troop sneered, and then turned and walked across the road with his little following to the next shop. There were policemen at the crossroads. They respectfully greeted the saffron bandanas.

Jamaal did not realize he was weeping until Kamaal sahib came up to him and suggested that he should go for a tea break. But Jamaal could only sit there and weep for the hopes he had had and the future he had seen.

Maybe it was his education that was to blame. He should never have studied history. In the textbooks he had read, it was a subject of hope, of promises and dreams. When he and countless others like him read Indian history in school, they often thought, for this was what they were encouraged to think, as we were before them: 'Now we are free. Now is our time. Now the world will see.'

It wasn't that poverty and pain, oppression and corruption were forgotten, his teacher at St Jude's had said, but after so long being the slaves of the English, any dawn when the sun did not rise on British lands was a good one. And tomorrow could only be better than yesterday; that was what the history books promised.

Jamaal saw that day what his tomorrow would be. He could see himself taking out the money and putting it into the tin without protest, grateful for being spared any damage and harm. It would not matter if he earned as little as he did or, after the fabled IIM MBA, earned a king's ransom. He knew that he didn't have the strength to oppose this, challenge those men not much older than him, and the state would look at him from across the street, dressed in official khaki, and pay its respects to his intimidators. There was no place to which he could flee. This was his home. Wherever he went, it would go with him.

Another man in his position might have recovered soon enough, or plotted vague revenge and carried on. But Jamaal lost all hope that day and a heavy weight crushed his heart. He found himself gasping, and turned his face to the wall so Kamaal sahib would not see him.

And then, when the pain lessened, he felt that it had swept away blockages in his heart and his mind, and another part of him was shouldering its way through. That evening, when he was sitting in his house, listening to the usual sounds of the street getting busy before the silence of another night, Jimmy the terrorist rose up within him and walked to the kitchen. He took the knife out of the drawer, the old knife that he remembered so well, and he stuck it next to himself in the old way. The metal was cold against his skin for a moment, and then it remembered its home.

Maybe the knife would have been the end of it. Jamaal would have walked to work with Jimmy the terrorist hidden within him, clutching the knife, the grip weakening day by day. Once in a while a certain word, a certain sentence would have brought Jimmy the terrorist rising up into Jamaal's eyes, only to withdraw, disappointed or diffident. It could not have lasted long. Jamaal was getting older, and some of his contemporaries in town had even married. Or he might have actually cleared the MBA exam. Ambition or domesticity would have dulled his anger, leeched it. And in the delight of his children he would in some years have forgotten Jimmy, the man who had appeared, fully formed, inside him that ordinary evening.

It was not meant to be.

Jamaal went to see a movie instead. It was *Bandit Queen*, based on the life of Phoolan Devi—you remember her? The lower-caste dacoit who came through horror to become a politician? Jamaal had not been able to summon the energy to watch it the first time it was shown, despite the controversy surrounding it. He hadn't the stomach, then, for gritty stories from his backyard. He did now—at least he was confused and angry enough to attempt it, almost as an act of defiance. The film was being shown at one of the cheaper movie theatres this time; it wouldn't be much of a loss if he did not like it.

It could be that other things were working too, who knows? There are those who believe that Fate stalks every life, forcing us, without us knowing, onto the paths we take. But if we must believe in Fate, then why should there be only one? A hundred thousand destinies could be stalking humanity, picking and choosing, raising up and discarding. It could be that more than one Fate works on a single person—and what happens if their separate interests collide? What happens to the puppet when the puppeteers clash? That's a question for us to ponder.

The movie was a rebirth for Jamaal. A harsh story, brutally told, it dragged him out from a decade of snivelling self-absorption. The pain that had allowed him to believe that he was somewhat special was rendered petty and shallow, and for the first time since he had hidden under his bed for fear of the mobs that never came, Jamaal saw someone else's pain.

He couldn't accept it. When Phoolan was being raped, the second time in the film, or the third, with matter-of-fact, mechanical violence in the drab and broken countryside, Jamaal rose and blindly staggered out of the theatre.

The air was chill and cleared his mind for a moment, and then he saw the policemen and the woman.

He didn't have to be told that she was a prostitute; there are things even an unworldly young man in a small town learns to tell. It probably would not have mattered much to him if he had known that the violence being inflicted on her was nothing to the woman; her uncle had inflicted much greater punishment when he forced her into the trade at age thirteen. This was only friendly persuasion, and it was a result of her own mistake. She had heard that there were customers to be had where this particular movie was being shown. Men came out wanting sex, and she had heard that they took pleasure in pain, but she needed the money. She should have realized, though, that every area has its own predators, and these policemen were not the usual ones she paid off.

It was the inspector who saw Jamaal first. He was not so focused on the woman and had left the task of her education to his two juniors. As befitted a man of his rank, Inspector Rawat merely watched and directed the beating and threats of rape. Jamaal's exit from the theatre had been covered by the noise of the movie running inside the hall. This was not one of those posh places with soundproof walls, and the doors had been left open; but as Jamaal stepped into the light the policeman saw him out of the corner of his eye and turned.

Rawat was somewhat bored, and a little frustrated. He owed his superiors some money and he had thought that the woman would have something for him, but the little whore had nothing except pleas for mercy. The young man coming out of the movie theatre became a natural target of his irritation.

'What do you think you're looking at, *gaandu*?' he said to Jamaal, and then leered, 'You want a little?'

Jamaal spat. It did not come out exactly how he had

anticipated, his mouth was too dry with sudden rage, and the spittle sprayed across the inspector's face.

The inspector did not react for a few second; he was that surprised. The two constables had turned at the sound of his voice, and now were stock-still. When Rawat finally spoke, wiping his face, his voice was clear and unruffled.

'Chaudhri, Kumar, see that the *haraamzaada* doesn't escape,' he said to his men, and then addressed Jamaal in a soothing, even loving, voice, 'Now, my little one, let us see about you.'

As they moved to hem Jamaal in, Rawat said, again in a soft, affectionate tone, 'Tell me your name, son.'

Jamaal should have run then. He was young, and fast. It is possible that he would have got away. This had all been a mistake. He was not one to start trouble, he could do something, he could escape. But the Fates rode him at that moment, and the knife that he always carried stirred next to his skin.

He moved so fast that Kumar and Chaudhri would swear later that Jamaal must have already been carrying the knife in his hand.

'*Maadarchod!*' Jimmy shouted as the cheap work of wood and steel found a home. As the blade sank into the inspector's khaki-covered belly, he yelled, 'My name is Jimmy the terrorist.'

The policemen gaped, and then Chaudhri struck. He brought his lathi down hard on Jamaal's wrist, fracturing the brittle bones in his fury and fear. Kumar moved soon after, recovering from his shock, and brought up his own lathi.

They beat him down until he could not stand, and then they kicked him, shattering teeth, tearing skin and rupturing organs with their boots. At some point Jamaal flopped into unconsciousness, and a sharp kick broke his neck. They went on kicking him long after he was dead, and Jimmy the terrorist with him.

It was only the whimper of the inspector that brought them back to their senses, after close to half an hour, after a lifetime of retribution. Rawat was sitting on the pavement with the knife protruding out of his belly. When Jamaal was struck down, the force had wrenched the knife out a little way and now the blood was spreading. The inspector had been in shock for those long minutes of Jamaal's death, but when the blood drenched his pants and invaded his underwear the sensation brought a mewl of fear out of him.

Three weeks later Inspector Rawat received an award for valour from the chief minister as he sat up painfully in the hospital bed.

No one asked who Jamaal had been, where he was born, or what he did, but Jimmy the terrorist was listed, his death reported, and maybe that is the important thing.

EPILOGUE

That is the official story.

There is, though, another version, the whore's version.

She says that after Jamaal stabbed the inspector, Kumar and Chaudhri fled. Jamaal looked at the inspector sitting shocked on the pavement, and putting one foot on Rawat's belly, he wrenched the blade out. Wiping it on the inspector's shirt, he tucked it back into his sleeve, the metal warm and sated.

She says that by the time Chaudhri and Kumar came back, Jimmy the terrorist was long gone, swallowed by the alleys of the Moazzamabad that bore him.

Author's Note

Every story has a story behind it. I first wrote 'Jimmy the Terrorist' as a short story in 2002/3 when I was living in Washington DC, finishing a Master's thesis, and both missing and dreading India. Missing it because I had not been back since 2001, dreading it because a few years out of the country had made me rethink the challenges we face. It was at this time that I started writing little vignettes and character sketches to put a human face to those challenges. 'Jimmy . . .' as a short story was my attempt to understand how our recent history of riots and curfews might affect an anonymous young man growing up in North India.

During those days I used to play chess (very badly) with an old school friend, Vamsee Kanchi, and talking about my writing during a game I said to him, 'Maybe that's just the fate of people.' To this Vamsee said, 'Why are we so fixated on one fate, maybe there are many?' Presumably he was just trying to distract me, since his chess skills were only marginally better than mine. But the idea stuck, and is possibly one of the keys to my later writing: that many fates are possible, and that people who report on stories, and tragedies, as if they were predestined somehow deprive us of the whole truth.

A couple of years ago I put all those vignettes together and tried to get it marketed as a collection of short stories called *Unbelonging*. Ravi Singh at Penguin India came back to me and said of 'Jimmy . . .', 'There's a lot happening in this story, would you want to make it into a novella or a novel?' In a collection, he said, it would be lost. Sabah Hamid, who is always the last court of appeals for me when it comes to things like this, said, 'No.' She really liked the short story, and thought I would only ruin it. Nandini Mehta, again somebody whose literary judgement I respect, also thought that the short story should not be stretched.

But I really wanted to write a longer story on similar issues, so I realized I would have to write a completely new one. Jimmy and the setting could not be anonymous; everything had to be detailed. Jimmy had to be a person in the real world, and this needed a family, a neighbourhood, a history.

There is a line in Frank Herbert's sci-fi classic *Dune* that has stayed with me—'Still, but one must ask: What is the son but an extension of the father?' So for me the book also became at least as much, if not more, about Jimmy's father. And for this, I turned to my own father for his memories of the 1960s, '70s and '80s. My father enjoyed his life thoroughly, and it is maybe his zest, his love of poetry that is captured in the early chapters of the book, although I have, as a darker person, drawn a darker picture of the times. (Perhaps there are other intimates and friends who have inspired parts of the book. I remember that my sister, reading the first draft, wondered which characters I had drawn from our extended family, because some of the words and actions seemed slightly familiar.)

A whole host of friends helped me, and commented on the manuscript. I am most indebted to two of them: Neha Kumar and Mandavi Mehta, who argued in detail about pretty much every single sentence of the book. In no particular order of preference, others whose comments, reading and advice shaped the novel are: Mushir Ahmad, Ateeq bhaijaan, Atika, Amitabha Bagchi, Ratika Kapur, Anuya Upadhyay, Vatsala Kaul Bannerjee, Mitali Saran, Kalyani Prasher, Hartosh Singh Bal, Rajeev Srivastava, Elena Bratanova, Basharat Peer and Rachna Kalra.

I have been exceedingly lucky in my friends.

I have been exceedingly lucky in my publishers as well. Mike Bryan, as CEO of Penguin India, was a wonderful source of support and enthusiasm, and Heather Adams made a particular remark after reading the first draft that made me realize I was still stuck in the short story and had some major changes to do before it became the novel I wanted it to be. Of course the most important editor of the whole thing was Ravi Singh, who long-sufferingly went through iteration after iteration of the manuscript before it was finally ready. The whole team at Penguin India has been a pleasure to work with, supportive, cheerful and very ready to help.

In the end I showed the manuscript to Sabah. And although she still loves the original story, she didn't disapprove. I guess I'll have to live with that.